PENGUIN BOOKS
# CONCERNING VIRGINS

Clare Boylan was born and grew up in Dublin, which is the setting for two of her novels. An award-winning journalist, she turned to fiction, enjoying widespread success with her short stories, which have been adapted into films and published in many countries as well as in her collection *A Nail on the Head*. After a career that has included playwriting, radio and television broadcasting, close-harmony singing, editing two magazines, bookselling and cutting the heads off cabbages in the back room of a grocery shop, she now confines herself to short and long fiction, cats, literary criticism and some journalism. Her three previous novels, *Holy Pictures*, *Last Resorts* and *Black Baby*, are also published by Penguin.

Clare Boylan lives in Wicklow with her journalist husband.

# CONCERNING VIRGINS

*A collection of short stories*

by

## CLARE BOYLAN

PENGUIN BOOKS

PENGUIN BOOKS

Published by the Penguin Group
27 Wrights Lane, London W8 5TZ, England
Viking Penguin Inc., 40 West 23rd Street, New York, New York 10010, USA
Penguin Books Australia Ltd, Ringwood, Victoria, Australia
Penguin Books Canada Ltd, 2801 John Street, Markham, Ontario, Canada L3R 1B4
Penguin Books (NZ) Ltd, 182–190 Wairau Road, Auckland 10, New Zealand

Penguin Books Ltd, Registered Offices: Harmondsworth, Middlesex, England

First published by Hamish Hamilton 1989
Published in Penguin Books 1990
1 3 5 7 9 10 8 6 4 2

'You Don't Know You're Alive' first appeared in *Living*
'The Picture House' first appeared in the *Irish Times* and *Cosmopolitan*
'Affairs in Order' first appeared in *Good Housekeeping*
'Technical Difficulties and the Plague' first appeared in *Perspective*
'L'Amour' first appeared in *Foreign Affairs* (anthology) and *Woman's Journal*
'Villa Marta' first appeared in the *Irish Times*
'The Miracle of Life' first appeared in *Cara* magazine
'A Model Daughter' first appeared in *Woman's Journal*
'Concerning Virgins' first appeared in *Image* magazine
and was read in the BBC's *Morning Story* series

Made and printed in Great Britain by
Richard Clay Ltd, Bungay, Suffolk

For Molly Keane

# Contents

# A Little Girl,
# Never Out Before

Mrs Deveney had a yellow face and lips like withered lupins. When she smiled her lips went down at the corners but the yellow ridges of her teeth stayed behind. Her eyes were like two tarnished salt spoons. She asked Frankie had she any religion and Frankie, echoing her mother, said that religion was for orphans and spinsters. She wanted to know what Frankie knew and Frankie said she couldn't say until she was asked. After that Mrs Deveney went mad entirely. 'You are an ignorant rip,' she told the little girl, 'who may take herself back home to her heathen of a mother.'

'Yes ma'am,' Frankie said, relieved, but when Mrs Deveney had finished going mad and had spun little ropes of white spit between her teeth she told Frankie to get up the stairs to Lena who would show her where she was to sleep and tell her her duties.

After her husband's death Mrs Deveney had opened a rooming house. It gave her an interest in life, which was an interest in making money. She advertised board and residence, superior; piano: £1 weekly. She mentioned its suitability for honeymooners, its view of the cattle mart, a speciality of home-made brown bread. She made the bread herself. It was not so much brown as a sort of greenish yellow with a sourness which was her particular gift.

The actual work of the house was done by a cook and

kitchen maid. She gave these girls time off for their religious duties and warm washing water every Saturday, but her goodness was wasted. A week before she had to get rid of Brid Feeney (with her big backside, like a married woman's) when she found her sitting on the edge of Mr McMahon's bed – a teacher – giving his back a scratch. It was not the suggestiveness of the situation that outraged her so much as the nerve of a serving girl making herself familiar with an educated man. It was the lack of proper deference to the male sex.

Brid Feeney only laughed at her; she said it wasn't the dark ages, it was the turn of the century. Mrs Deveney disliked the phrase. It made her think of milk on the turn. The world was turning bad. The past decades had brought flying machines, motor cars, electric lighting, defying the laws of nature and flying in the face of God. She still believed in the old ways, in sentimental values.

She found the little girl through a notice in *Freeman's Journal*. Up to this she had taken girls sent to her by the nuns but the sisters had a redemptive mission and she had a suspicion that they caught their girls in the act of falling. There was something wordly and sniggering about them. They lacked the humility that was proper to the poor.

When she applied herself to the newspaper columns, therefore, she was looking for something more than a kitchen maid. She was seeking a phrase, a niceness.

'A rabbit trapper – has been brought up to it. Highest references from gentleman.' 'Mrs Harford will teach new beginners the pianoforte.' 'Good cook, thoroughly understands her business.' Lena's hard toast crackled beneath Mrs Deveney's porcelain teeth and she softened it wistfully with a mouthful of tea. Downstairs she could hear that same horse of a one bawling that Jesus Mary and Joseph she only had one pair of hands as some

couple from the country complained of having to go
hungry on their honeymoon.

'An orphan (16) from school, wishes to go to a lady
where she would be taught to be a servant;' and then –
'A respectable little girl, never out before.'

She explored the notion of herself as a lady but then
she thought, sixteen was very old for an orphan to be
looking for work. Already she had probably left a brace
of triplets in some other orphanage.

She liked the idea of a little girl, never out before. She
pictured something as new and unprinted as the Holy
Communion wafer, unspoilt, unknowing, modest, and
cheap.

The little girl turned out small for her age. She said
she was twelve but looked not more than ten. Her
brown pinafore had a lifeless look, which was common
to the clothing of the poor and came not, as people
imagined, from infrequent washing but from insufficient
rinsing as water had to be carried up from a yard and
the whole wash was rinsed in a single tub. She folded
her hands in front of her but they kept unfolding and
grasping at air as if she was used to holding a doll.

Lena showed her the wooden box where she was to
keep her underwear and her shoes and a nail on the wall
for her coat. There was a wardrobe but it was full of
Lena's things – clothes and boxes and romantic novel-
ettes. A basin of cold water was left on top of the wooden
box for weekday washing but Lena said she never
washed until Saturdays, except her hands which Mrs D
inspected twenty times a day.

Lena complained that Mrs D expected them to strip
down to their raw bones every night and then undress in
the morning again for washing but she herself kept her
underwear on day and night as the cold was brutal. She
advised Frankie to do the same as she didn't want to

have to look at her raw bones. Since Lena looked like a fat white fish with pendulums of flesh adorning her jaws and tiny rows of greasy brown ringlets, Frankie was quite agreeable to this arrangement.

The cook was an immense country girl of twenty-two or three. She moved slowly and had small brown eyes. When she recited the litany of rough work that was to fill Frankie's days, the little girl couldn't help thinking it left hardly anything at all for Lena herself to do. All the same the cook had a secret which Frankie recognized right away. In the disappointing house she would wear it against her chest like a locket.

'Get up at 6.30 winter, six o'clock in summer, open shutters, light range, lay breakfast tables, sweep and dust drawing room and supply all rooms with coal,' Lena recited. 'Clean all the flues, black lead kitchen range, wash out kitchen boiler, clean thoroughly the hall, kitchen stairs, passages and water closets. Take cans of hot water to every room. Empty slops.' Lena showed Frankie the house as she reeled off the kitchen maid's responsibilities. Frankie appraised gaunt curtains in the cheerless colours of dried blood or dried peas, the mismatched furniture and pictures of stags or saints bleeding on the walls.

'Never go into the boarders' rooms without knocking,' Lena warned her. 'There's married couples in some.'

'I know all about that,' Frankie was glad to know something, although it would be hard not to know when you lived in one room with your ma and da and the young ones.

'Maybe you know too much.' Lena folded her arms. 'Maybe you think you're Miss Hokey Fly eighteen ninety-nine. Well let me put this in your pipe. It's me be's in charge round here and if anything is took or stole, it's you'll be blempt.'

The older girl went out into the back yard and leaned against a lavatory shed with a festering smell. She hummed a tune that was popular in Dan Lowry's. 'Have you your women's monthlies yet?' Frankie nodded. 'Mine have went,' Lena remarked, 'but they were a nuisance.' She was disappointed that the new girl was only a child. She seemed too young even for teasing. 'What are you thinking, Hokey Fly?'

'The house,' Frankie said. 'It isn't much, is it?'

'What were you expecting, uniformed butlers and electrical lights?'

She had been expecting a garden with asters and dahlias, an apple tree.

The child gave her the pickle, Lena decided, with her delicate lady's air and her rotten span of attention. 'Have you got any questions, Hokey, or do you know it all by now?'

She plucked back her attention from an upstairs window where a long-faced woman stood fastening the throat of an opossum cape. 'Do we get much to eat?' she said.

The little girl sat on the edge of the bed in the dark, her blanket wrapped around her shoulder, her bare legs dangling over the edge. Unknown to sun or sky, it was morning. She had slept a little towards dawn, a dizzy sickly doze, and then woken in a panic because the baby was missing. She always slept with it in her arms and they woke up wet but warm. In the day she carried the infant while she cleaned up or cooked and her hands were formed to its support.

When she opened her eyes she thought she was at home because of the loud, gurgling snores that were like her da's but it was Lena. Lena was who she lived with now. She wondered when she'd ever see her ma again, or cuddle the baby. Ah, she missed her ma. She cried for a few minutes, wiping her eyes and nose with her blanket, but Lena reached out her big knobby foot and gave her a kick so she pulled on her brown pinafore and her stockings and boots and went down to light the range.

Her room was in the attic of the house and she crept down its five storeys in the dark, past the snuffling creaking married couples, past the yearning schoolteacher and the long-faced woman with the opossum cape, past the dark dining room and drawing room which waited in silence to claim life from her fidgeting hands.

The cold possessed her like a drowning. She felt her way to the kitchen and stood there in the dark. Lena had not shown her where to find matches. Who can tell what hides in the dark of old kitchens, scuttling about with mice and mould and skins of dripping? The sounds that live inside total silence are the worst in the world. She crept around, her fingers touching things that felt horrible – soaking porridge, tea leaves in a sieve. Her breath came out in persevering grunts. At last she grasped a match and lit the kitchen lamp. It leaked a little pool of yellow light and monsters swarmed up the wall. She knelt on the floor and began to rake out the ashes.

It was her mother's idea that she should go to work in a big house. They were pals. They comforted each other with sweet tea and the flesh of babies. Her da was always after her ma, all the time. They could have stopped him, disabled him with a knife or a chair, but they had a weakness. They both loved infants, newborn. No matter that there wasn't even enough for the existing ones to eat, Frankie and her ma saw infants as the marvel of the world. It was worth all the hurting and the hunger to have another, brand new, every other year.

They were a hopeless pair, she and her ma. When her father had gone out for the day and the middle ones were in school Frankie would climb back into bed beside her. They kept themselves warm with the two little ones. They dreamed of the feasts they might eat if there was ever any money, but they didn't bother all that much. Hunger was just a fact of their life, and there were rewards.

It was after Frankie got her women's monthlies that the notion arose of sending her away. She was growing into a lady now, her ma said. It was time to learn a lady's life.

Her ma said that she would learn the quality of fine silver and how to stitch linen. She would eat blancmange and cold beef in the kitchen. She would gather roses in a wicker basket and arrange them on a polished table by a long window. It became their new dream, after the dreams of food. In idle fancy they walked under wedding-cake ceilings, exploring the rooms, peeking into bureaux to spy on love letters, opening the lids of golden boxes to admire jewels or bon bons or cigars inside. They mooned over the young man of the house who was kind but distant, concealing emotion beneath a brittle moustache as he played at the piano.

She didn't look any more like a lady than she had the year before. Her legs were sticks and her chest was flat as a wash board. All the same she was growing up and her father knew it too. Sometimes when he came in from his night's drinking and had performed gravely in the bucket in the corner, he would reach not for Ma but for Frankie, his dimmed senses directed by nostalgia to the spring scent of womanhood and not its spent season.

She stuffed the stove's ugly gob with coke and papers and stood over it while it lit, shivering and warming her legs as she tempted it with morsels of twisted paper and a sprinkling of sugar the way her mother had shown her. By the time it was lighting the kitchen clock said a quarter past seven and she had to run to catch up. There was no time to wash her hands when she finished the fires so that the breakfast plates and saucers were branded by her black prints as she set the tables.

In all their uncertain fantasies of grandeur the one thing Frankie and her ma had been sure of was that there would be enough to eat in a big house. Poor Ma wouldn't believe it if she told her she had nothing since her tea yesterday, which was two slices of the sour brown bread smeared with marge. There would be no more until after the boarders had eaten breakfast, when she could have some of the porridge that remained.

The poor learn to live with hunger by moving slowly and sleeping a lot but she had hardly slept and she had to run all the time to keep up with the work. As she set out the bread and sausages and rings of black pudding for Lena to cook for breakfast, her fingers fell to temptation and stealthily fed her a slice of bread. After that she went upstairs to knock up the married couples.

Mrs Deveney was pleased with the little girl's first day. She wasn't sociable. She did not look at the male boarders nor loiter on the landings with Lena. In spite of her dreamy air, she was thorough. Her fires did not go out. An inspection of the dishes she washed revealed no scabs of oatmeal, no rusty stains of tea. She summoned Frankie after she had finished making the beds and emptying the slops. The child looked dazed. Her face was a panic-stricken white and her hands black as the devil. 'What are you?' Mrs Deveney asked her briskly.

'I'm a girl.' Frankie looked surprised. 'A maid.' She knew nothing. She had answered wrong. She waited patiently while the lupin lips wove themselves into a shape for contumely.

'You are a filthy, thieving little tinker of the common lower orders,' Mrs Deveney said.

Frankie looked at the big black piano, as fat and listless as a funeral horse. She wondered if the boarders ever dared to use it, if one of the silent men at breakfast might serenade his new wife, while she leaned across the lid to show him her breasts.

*Oft in the stilly night* . . . Her mother used to sing that long ago. She wondered what her ma was doing now. Was the baby fretting for her?

'Look at me!' snapped Mrs Deveney. 'Explain yourself.'

A bag of bones her da used to say, until she began to turn into a lady. A flock of dreams. A waking ghost. A gnaw of hunger.

'You left filthy black fingerprints all over the breakfast china and you stole a slice of bread.'

'I was hungry,' Frankie said, and then, invaded by curiosity; 'how did you know?'

'The nerve of you! Every stim in this house is counted. The bread is cut the night before – two slices for every boarder. It was Lena who informed me of the robbery.'

Mrs Deveney demanded to know why Frankie had not worn gloves while doing the dirty work of the house, the grates and the slops, and declared that she had brought a breath of depravity into a good Catholic household. She believed it too but did not add that it was a matter of routine. All the servants stole. She expected it and kept their rations meagre knowing that thieving was in their nature and that they would steal food whether they needed it or not.

In a matter of weeks Frankie would grow cunning and learn to conceal evidence of her enterprise. Lena was by now an accomplished bandit. Search as she might Mrs Deveney could only find clues to modest pilferage yet the girl grew fatter by the hour.

Was ever a slice of bread so richly mourned? The little salt-spoon eyes seemed to corrode yet further as rebuke buzzed from the withered lips. And still she was hungry. She thought about the newest baby, Doris, whose eyes were not like salt spoons but like measured sips of a morning sky. At first those eyes had been blind and it was her little ruched mouth that pondered but in a little while everything was lit up by their wonder as if they saw the face of God, if you believed in that sort of thing, or a fairy.

Jack was next, named by their father after the boxer Jack Kilraine, the Terror of the Age, but their Jack was only two and had not yet fulfilled his father's hopes, having a preference for sweetened milk and women's bodies. There was Ethel and Mick, aged six and ten. Frankie loved them all and felt gratified by their need of her. She was proud to be her mother's protector. She had no desire for an independent life. Her own needed her. They always would. She thought of them all alone, with no one to comfort them or cook for them, and panic gripped at her knees. Who would cheer her ma up in the morning after her da had gone, leaving the trail of his temper, a smell of beer and the dank aftermath of his night-time business?

She always lay on the bed looking cold and sort of grey until Frankie brought her tea and opened the windows and sang a few songs and lit up the ashes in the grate.

Christmas was only six weeks off and the small ones were already counting. Frankie was the one who made the ginger biscuits and scrounged for oranges to put in the children's stockings. It was she who saved up new pennies, one for each child.

'I'm going home now,' she said in her offhand way. 'My ma will be wanting me.'

'Ah, now,' the widow looked alarmed. 'Your

mammy is depending on the few shillings. You'd only be letting her down.'

'No I wouldn't,' Frankie said. 'My ma loves me.'

'Of course she does,' Mrs Deveney forced her mouth down into a smile. 'You're only in want of refinement and religion. You should pin your hair up and maybe I'd make you a present of a gown for Sundays. Brid Feeney's grey could be cut down for you. I'm going to give you time off to go to Mass and confession with Lena. What do you say?'

Frankie shook her head. She was too tired. She only wanted to go home.

'And if you were loyal to me, of course, you would get a nice present at Christmas – something you could bring home to benefit your poor little brothers and sisters. Say "yes ma'am".' Her smile vanished when she saw ambition enter Frankie's dreamy eye. 'Say "thank you, ma'am".'

She got used to the wearing of household gloves, the smell of chloride of lime and the racking bouts of grief that she carried carefully to the outside lavatory. She learned to steal things that could not be counted, spoons of starch or custard powder, a fistful of dry oatmeal.

The married couples came and went, their honeymoons accomplished with relief, if not much comfort. McMahon the schoolteacher stayed on. Sometimes he invited Frankie into his room, but she said she wasn't allowed. The boys who came to the back door with fish or groceries tried to grapple with her but she was a good kicker. Anyway, they preferred Lena who developed a kind of glamour in the hands of men, allowing them to feel her giant bosoms or anything they liked.

Once she surprised her in the pantry with a bakery lad. The youth and the massive girl turned to gawp at her. 'Get out! Get away you dirty little scut, you cur,' Lena snarled.

'You'll get a baby if you do that,' Frankie told her.

'Don't you be ridiculous,' Lena said. 'How could I get a baby now?'

Frankie laughed, which earned her a blow on the ear. There was no argument to that.

Within a month she had begun to turn into one of those wiry little workers, who are silent and swift and indispensable. Mrs Deveney kept her word and came up the five flights of stairs, carrying, with caution and difficulty, her Christmas gift.

It was a little house or shed. The roof was thatched like those of the poor cottagers who lived in the hills, and animals wandered around inside. A poor little baby slept in a pigsty or something.

'What is it?' Frankie said. She had been hoping for money or a box of biscuits, something for the children.

'It is the holy crib,' Mrs Deveney stood back to let the child peer inside the house where she saw that there were toy people as well as animals and the baby. Foreigners. 'What's it for?' she said.

'It is to put you in mind of the spirit of Christmas,' the widow mystifyingly declared. 'The figure in the manger is baby Jesus and the lady in blue is His mother, the Virgin Mary.'

'She can't be His mother,' Frankie said; 'not if she's a virgin.'

'These are the three wise kings, led to Bethlehem by a star shining from the East, who came to worship and brought gold, frankincense and myrrh.'

'Who were they?' Frankie wondered.

'They were gifts!' Mrs Deveney tried to hide her impatience of the little girl's stupidity, for it was all as plain to her as right and wrong, but her teeth clenched and she sprayed spit. 'Gifts of inestimable value. Lena will explain.'

But all Lena explained was that Jesus Mary and Joseph they had enough junk in the room already. She picked up the little house just as Frankie was examining a mouse-sized ox. She climbed on to her own bed and heaved the crib up on top of the wardrobe.

One Sunday at Mass the little girl grew bored and slipped out of church and used the halfpenny she had been given for the collection plate to go home on a tram. She didn't have to worry about Lena, who never went to Mass anyway but loitered under a big-brimmed hat talking to corner boys.

It was a shock when she saw their room again, so cluttered, so cold. Had it always been so mingy? She stood in the doorway, looking at these poor people, trying to make them her own.

Her ma was the first to notice her. She sat up in bed, tears filling her eyes, unable to speak but silently mouthing, 'Frankie, Frankie.' She seemed astonished to see her as if she had imagined her dead or gone for ever.

'Hello, Ma,' Frankie said. 'I've come home. I'll stay if you want.'

'Ah, Frankie!' her mother found her voice. 'Aren't you a picture?'

Frankie's bones hurt from wanting to be squeezed. She wanted to run to her ma, but she couldn't, there was a restraint. She decided to make herself useful and bent before the cold fire, shovelling out the ash, putting aside any useful lumps of coke.

'Ah God!' her mother cried, 'your lovely dress! Get up, Ethie,' she nagged the younger child. 'Your sister's used to better now.'

Ethel sidled past Frankie in her greyish petticoat. She was carrying Doris. 'She's wet,' she said, and would not let her go when Frankie tried to take the baby.

'I amn't changed,' Frankie said. 'I never stopped thinking about you – every minute of every day.'

Her ma was out of bed now, pulling on her clothes. She kept having to sniff back tears. She snorted with her head stuck in the neck of her jumper.

'Da?' Frankie appealed.

Her father nodded at her politely and pulled up his blanket to cover his vest.

She wanted to hold them all, even her da. They were trying to do things for her. They cleared clothes off a chair so that she could sit down. Ethel put a cup of tea in her hand and her mother spread a tea towel over her knee. 'To save your lovely dress,' she said.

'It's not mine,' she said. 'I only wear this of a Sunday. Mrs Deveney cut it down from the last girl. Underneath, I'm still the same.'

Her mother shook her head. 'You look the part, so you do.'

Ethel fingered the grey grosgrain bow which Mrs Deveney took from a box each Sunday morning to pin to the back of Frankie's hair. 'Can you get me one of those?' she said.

'You can have this one,' Frankie said, knowing she would be killed when she went back, if she went back.

To the family, her carelessness with ribbons was more evidence of her social success. 'Tell us dotey,' her mother said; 'what's it like, the big house?'

She would tell Mrs Deveney that a boy stole her bow outside the church – a Protestant boy.

What would she say to her mother? 'There's a garden,' she improvised. 'Roses and apples – a strawberry bed.'

'What do you eat?' her ma said. 'Do you eat strawberries?'

'Chicken,' she decided.

'You'd never fit in with us now,' her mother nodded, confirming for herself the worst. 'Not any more.'

'I would so,' Frankie said.

'You'd never fit anyhow,' her father grinned. 'Your mother hasn't told you yet. We've another one on the way.'

Frankie's ma held on to Ethel for comfort.

In the afternoon, back in the big house, the ache in her bones became a squealing. None of them had hugged her. They clutched at her Sunday gloves as she said goodbye. She helped Lena with the dinner and cleared the tables and then the Sunday afternoon silence descended and she was alone. She went up to the second landing and knocked on the door of McMahon, the schoolteacher. He closed the door behind them. While he felt around under her clothes, she watched herself in the mirrored door of his wardrobe. She could see that they were right. She was different. The dreamy look had gone from her eyes. Her legs were getting a shape of their own. Even her chest, which the schoolteacher smoothed with chalky fingers, had developed a springy feel. With her hair up her face looked strange. They'd never leave her alone now. She was pretty.

She felt no better afterwards, although no worse, and went outside for a cry in the lavatory. When she emerged into the yard a big lumpy cat was sitting on the wall, looking down at her. 'You're in trouble,' she noticed, 'ain't you?' She held out her arms and the animal made a leap that looked suicidal but the child managed to catch it. 'They won't let me keep you,' Frankie told the creature, but the rumbling warmth relieved her aching arms. She carried it upstairs. There was nowhere to hide it so she stood on the bed as Lena had done and hoisted the cat up into the Christmas crib.

That night when she was damping down the fires, a terrible bawling came from her room. Frankie flew up the stairs, her boots barely grazing the steps. Lena must have found the cat. She must be having a fit.

She wasn't having a fit. Frankie grinned when she saw the fat girl stranded on the bed, her ringlets pinned to her wet red forehead and howls flying from her mouth like bats from a cave. She was having her baby.

'I'm poisoned. I'm dyin'' Lena gasped.

'You're all right,' Frankie dabbed at Lena's forehead with the end of her pinafore. 'Your baby's coming.'

Lena stopped bawling to gape at her. 'What are you on about?'

'You can't keep it hid no more,' Frankie said. 'I knew from the first minute I saw you, you was having a baby.'

'You know nothing! You're just pig ignorant,' Lena whimpered. 'How could I be having a baby an' I not even married?'

'Don't you have no brothers and sisters?' Frankie began to tear up her sheet. 'Ain't you never seen your mam havin' a baby?'

'I be's from the orphanage,' Lena said. 'I can't be havin' a baby. I bein't married.'

Frankie sighed. 'Take long breaths and try not to make a racket. I'll tell ma'am you've got a colic.'

Mrs Deveney sat up in bed plucking the beads of her rosary as if tearing leeches from her flesh. 'Lena is poorly, ma'am, but she don't need a doctor,' Frankie said.

'No,' Mrs Deveney said; 'no doctor. She is as strong as a horse.'

After four hours a baby boy came. Puce and mummified the infant gave a thrilling cry and Frankie washed him in the bucket of warm water she had dragged up from the kitchen and laid him on her pillow. When she had him settled she turned to comfort Lena and saw that the girl was in labour again. Close to morning a little girl came and the needling cry was answered by a bird from the dawn roofs.

For a long time Frankie could only stare at them. No humans could be so perfect, so perfectly matched. They even had hair, black and silky thistledown tufts. Although she hadn't slept all night, their creamy sleep restored her. She lay down for a little while beside them on the bed and then she went downstairs to light the range.

She had to make the breakfasts herself that morning and clear up after them so it was ten o'clock before she could get back upstairs with tea for Lena.

Lena was gone. The bloody rags and bucket were gone. The babies were missing.

At lunchtime, when the cook returned, she climbed into bed in all her clothes and sullenly stared at the wall.

'Where are the babies?' Frankie said.

'What babies?' Lena heaved around to face her. 'I was poisoned by a bad sassidge. I been to the doctor and he said to stay in bed.'

'Twins,' Frankie said. 'I washed them myself and put them on my bed.'

'Well there be's no twins now and no bucket neither and you better stop behaving like a demented herrin'.'

'I didn't mention the bucket,' Frankie said.

Lena sat up in bed and screeched at her. 'There was no bucket!'

And suddenly Frankie knew. She knew. She saw the little hands grasping at the bloody water, so familiar from their recent swimming home, the dark fronds of their hair rising to the oily surface to explore the air.

'I know there were babies,' she glanced around the room as if looking for a clue and her eyes came to rest on the cat in the crib, who had maintained her conspiracy of silence throughout the howling night. The cat kneaded the straw and blinked at her. 'Twins.'

'You know nothin', Hokey,' Lena said; 'and there bein't nothin' you can do about it neither.'

Downstairs Mrs Deveney was already up and scrubbing a bucket in the yard. She was giving out about Lena's idleness. She thought she might dispatch her back to the nuns. When she saw the way Frankie was looking at her, the yellow of her skin became tinged with ash. 'Go into the kitchen now and get yourself a little egg,' she said and dragged her lips down towards reluctant mirth.

A week after Lena went back to scrub for the nuns Frankie's cat gave birth to three kittens in the straw. She had never seen new-born kittens before. Their tiny paws, like blackberries, and blunt, bad-tempered snouts enchanted her. Her mother told her that people drown kittens in a bucket, but she didn't believe it. No one would do such a thing.

'Any road,' she told herself, 'I'll keep them hid.' Her employer seemed older since Lena's departure. Maybe she wouldn't bother with the long climb all the way up to the attic.

It was the little girl's first Christmas away from home. She couldn't leave. It wasn't just the kittens. With no other help in the house Mrs Deveney needed her.

She got two shillings from McMahon the schoolteacher and spent it on a basket of oranges with silver paper around the handle, and halfpennies hidden in the fruit. She sent this by messenger to her house, with a bottle of port for her ma and da.

In the morning she cooked the Christmas dinner for Mrs Deveney and McMahon, swathed in a big holland apron which showed off her waist. Afterwards she stole milk for the mother cat and a glass of sherry for herself and went upstairs to play with the kittens.

They kneaded their mother with the tiny thorns of their claws, tumbling on the bed where she had imagined twins to have proceeded from the beguiling fatness of

Lena the cook. She was all right now. Mrs Deveney got her violet powder for her nightmares.

She picked up the kittens and held them to her chest. They depended on her. She loved them more than all the world. She still knew nothing, but she was learning. Refinement and religion, you picked them up as you went along.

The three kittens were different colours – yellow, and striped and a black one swirled with white stars like the star that had led the wise men to Bethlehem with their gifts of inestimable value. She named them Gold and Frankincense and Myrrh.

## Venice Saved

He was in the gloomy outer bar of the Locanda Cipriani, dripping water on to the tiled floor from the bald top of his head and the mushy wads of a grey anorak when the woman walked out of the restaurant and stood by the window, watching rain spluttering at the glass. Orange gold and pastel pink, tiny feet in dainty shoes and skin of some opaque white bridal fabric, she stood perfectly still, clutching a little bag, her eyes as wistful as seawater.

His first instinct was relief and his reaction was to give thanks to God, for which he closed his eyes, squeezing out more water, which streamed down from his eyebrows. People who saw him thought he was crying and wondered if they should disturb him to tell him that the boat had arrived and it was time to leave, but he was too foreign, too exposed in his emotions. When he opened his eyes she was gone. He showed no surprise having already, at the age of twenty-seven, lost everything in his life except his money, to which there seemed no end.

He had come to Torcello in search of a virgin. The 'Vergine con Bambino Benedicente' in the cathedral was described as radiant, but when he plodded through the marshy grasses of that ruined island in a cloudburst, he saw at once that it was the golden mosaic which formed her setting that was radiant. She herself had been dimmed by loss. She looked like a widow or the mother of a dead child.

Venice – 'city of graceful walls and gleaming arcades, veined with azure and warmed with gold, and fretted with white sculpture like frost upon forest branches turned to marble'.

The Venice of Ruskin, with which he had armed himself against isolation on the train, sounded an austere place, pure and meticulous.

He had stepped out of the railway station into a light drizzle and there was the water, like a calamity. It was not clean as the mountain streams of home which splintered into diamonds on the stones, but a foetid broth that riled the air, and flipped slime into the hallways of palazzos. The buildings themselves had the overblown grandeur of a painted stage curtain and suffered a hideous parody in the lagoon's lapping jaw, which upended them and bobbed them on their heads.

Massoud was ill. He was a worry to the girls who had taken him on. He was sick to his soul. He grew up in the mountains of Lebanon but when war broke out his father had removed his two most precious possessions – his son and his money – for safekeeping to America, the land of the free. He lived in California now. It was rosy as an apple, but the core had been eaten by a worm. At first, the beautiful girls who chewed gum and played transistor radios ignored him and he was very lonely. He tried to find company among the fresh-faced young men in pastel sweaters but they seemed physically to exclude him, moving about their space so that there was nowhere for him to stand or sit down. He gave up his effort after a while, after he heard a group of them talking about Bob. 'Who's Bob?' someone wanted to know. 'Oh, he's Dick's boyfriend.'

In due course the girls began to examine him more closely. 'What do you *do*?' they said, hanging on to his wrist, to reveal to him the Rolex watch they had discovered there. They wore sunglasses with frames in the fluorescent colours of lollipops. Their clothes were short, tight tubes of thick black jersey, or very tight exercise suits in the same material, which made them look like human biros. They studied him with the directness of a very young child or a very old whore and he understood that they wanted to know not what he did but how he got his money.

'I'm in real estate,' he said.

'You sell houses?'

'No,' Massoud pedantically corrected. 'I buy them.'

After that they were with him wherever he went, shimmying and gnashing and shaking their hair. They dogged his trail, not like a harem for they did not belong to him, they owned him. They were in his bed and on the phone, stamping around him in night clubs, stuffing him with beansprouts and sushi. The girls he lay with lectured him about smoking and safe sex. They carried Tampax and condoms in little snappy bags that fastened with Velcro. They made him test for AIDS and wear a hat to protect his bald patch from the frayed ozone. In bed they rarely slept but ate Chinese food from cardboard boxes and watched television and held rap sessions, talking in monotones about their sex lives, their childhoods, their shrinks. They did not speak in English but some language they had invented which symbolized English.

Wisps of anecdote were offered without connecting verbs or directive themes, but the monologue was punctuated with their common query: 'You know?' If you said no, you did not know, they sighed and softly muttered 'Creep.' You were meant to say, 'Sure, sure.'

The patter of their voices fell like rain and sometimes he would turn his head away to silently weep. They never asked him why he wept but phoned one another, reporting in their low monotones punctuated by the occasional snap and squelch of gum. 'Sood is low.' 'What's the matter?' 'Who knows? He cries.'

Then they confronted him, all of them together, the girls whose beautiful breasts he tried to memorize in order to remember their names in bed, for their faces were difficult to distinguish. 'We're your *friends*,' they announced, as if he ought to have been suspicious. 'We want to help you. You have to tell us what's the matter.'

'I am unhappy,' he said.

'He's going to tell us his wives don't understand him,' said Laurelle or Lavelle.

'I need beauty,' he sullenly demanded.

'Beauty.' The one he thought was called Janine raised her eyebrows and shook her head.

The rest of the girls exchanged uneasy glances thinking he was criticizing them but then they grinned, they were perfect, they conformed. They had brought along a radio with separate speakers which supplied loud music with a background of crashing metal to avert the horror of possible silence. Their small bottoms bounced to its rhythm in private industry.

How beautiful was the stillness of woman. He longed for a woman with the skin of a petal, with a mouth that curved and shimmered and was still. The world was not divided into male and female in the way that people nowadays imagined, with equal rights, as if rights were a human and not divine dominion.

It was the stillness and the restlessness. As God made man, He compensated him. As God made woman, He gazed at her. There was no rest for man, unless it was in woman. She was the fount and the wellspring.

He thought of the women of his home who walked in shade, moving slowly and with grace, whose eyes were mystery. People called them oppressed but in his mind it was Western women who were oppressed, their faces creased with stress and ambition, their bodies muscled from running and jogging and attempting macramé with their limbs in order to achieve the satisfaction which was their due, in the transaction of making love.

The women he had known in his own country seemed to him complete. They harboured life. The men chivvied and herded them, fearful of their strength, and the women whispered potently among themselves.

It did not occur to the young American girls that despair might be proper to Massoud's plight. So long as you had bread, there was an answer to everything.

'Venice!' pronounced one who might be either Frannie or Zoe.

There was a brief bout of intensive chewing and then the others all nodded their heads. 'Venice!'

Not all of them had been there but everyone knew it was the most beautiful place in the world.

All the dogs were muzzled. They took their revenge by excreting softly and very centrally along the pavement. To avoid befouling one would have to step into the canal. Placing his new Italian shoes with care, Massoud was unable to look up at the domes and cupolas, the spires and golden beasts and bells. Instead his haunted eye picked out some fresh displeasure at the water's edge, a slimy form which seemed to contain a snarl. He was compelled to examine it and found that it was a dead rat, the rotting flesh peeled back to bone. No one else seemed to notice. It was a private horrifying encounter which engaged him until he was startled by a large black gondola gliding past his street corner. It was stuffed with Japanese men in suits, sitting bolt upright, looking wary and helpless like victims of a kidnap.

When he did look around all he could see were trudging Americans and more Japanese, slung about with cameras, beleaguered by cats, besmirched by pigeons. For a brief instant his eye found consolation in a smudge of pink in the distance, something that might be the petal of a rose, or a woman, a small form of singular grace which moved with composure and then vanished.

What place was he in? His hotel was called The Brooklyn. He could have afforded the Danieli, but the American girls put him in The Brooklyn because it was where people like themselves stayed and they could keep an eye on him. He wandered into a restaurant and was disconcerted when the menu told him that it was the Trattoria Sayonara.

Walking through a dark alley he was startled first by a glaring stone cherub caught in the chill halo of a night light that poked through a froth of leaves, and then by a diamond necklace which moved in its stealthy glow six inches above the ground.

Was it a woman who crawled about among the dogs' droppings in her evening wear on her belly? He would scarcely have been surprised. When it turned out to be a Siamese cat with a diamante-studded collar, he was hardly relieved. The city was infested with cats. He had had an earlier shock when crossing the Accademia Bridge his nose was assailed by a sharpish odour and looking down in the dusk he saw a thousand writhing creatures, snapping and scrapping and clawing at strands of cold spaghetti on pieces of paper. They were only cats, but sewer cats, and their knowing, exhausted eyes terrified him. When he leaned over the bridge to look at them they ceased their activity and peered back, their verveless eyes glinting like flies in the twilight. They were not pleading. They were waiting.

'Where am I?' he whispered.

It was a question that he was to repeat continually. He kept getting lost. He got off the vaporetta at the wrong end of the island or found himself dislocated by haunting images. When he went to the casino, which was housed in the Palazzo Loredan-Vendramin-Calergi, once occupied by Wagner, he was deposited at an ugly modern building miles away on the lido.

The palazzo was only the casino's winter quarters, he was told; he saw no reason to believe it.

Massoud found himself at a crap table where two fat American women in fur coats talked in loud voices as they tossed green counters on the baize. 'What do you think of electrolysis?' one said, and he strained to avoid hearing, but when this part of the conversation had been completed, the other called out: 'Do ya wax your lip?'

In Harry's Bar, he was diverted by a woman who looked like a toad (her dress, disturbingly, was toad-patterned silk, yellow on green) and who ate a dish of asparagus in a peculiar manner, feeding the stems into her mouth without punctuation, so that it seemed as a single length and she appeared to be eating a snake.

He had long understood that the West was unsaved. All the prophets came from the East – Jesus, Buddha, Mohammed. Around him the tourists exclaimed in rapture at the costly adornments of the buildings, the priceless paintings. Was it only he who saw a junk shop ruled by verminous birds and animals; an overweight charm bracelet sinking into mud? Others looked up to dazzling rooflines, frescoed ceilings. He himself became preoccupied with what was underneath. Had the city been flooded by engineers after the buildings were erected, or did slaves labour in stinking water, to sink wooden piles into the slime? He could not look on the drowning walls without imagining men working beneath them to root a city to the ocean floor. Had they died without seeing the gilded domes, the rampant nymphs and festive stucco? Were they in heaven now, feasting on magnificence, while the city was sinking into hell?

On one of his failed excursions Massoud came across an interesting bookshop close to Harry's Bar. He armed himself with a selection of Venetian guide books and reflections and withdrew from the chaos to sip fruit juice in Florian's while the violins sawed away in the drizzle.

He discovered that the walls of the city were not stitched with mud but with the corpses of saints. Lounging up against the stonework you might be in unwary contact with St Stephen's arm, St Philip's head, some tufts of flesh from the body of St Paul or even a tooth of John the Baptist. The rotting remains of St Mark had been smuggled in their pungent entirety to the city by two ninth-century merchants.

The alarm caused by this discovery was relieved by a revelation that others besides himself responded warily to the city's excesses. 'A stinkpot charged with the very virus of hell', one early visitor had recorded. Charles Dickens saw it as 'a very wreck found drifting in the sea'. Four times the city had been swept by plague. Other noisome epidemics arose from the fact that in the sixteenth century prostitutes numbered one tenth of the population.

The books also beguiled with individual descriptions and it was when he found the word 'radiant' that he went in search of the Madonna on Torcello.

The rain stopped briefly as he was sailing back from Torcello. He looked up as the boat slid beneath two stone lions and saw that the horizon was spiked by snowy peaks. 'What are they?' he spoke aloud. 'They're the Alps, pal,' said an American in unfriendly tones.

'But the Alps are in Switzerland,' Massoud warned. He
was so confused he missed his stop and debarked on the
Riva degli Schiavoni where the tourists are knotted like
a tumour and the air tightens with greed.

A fresh deluge made him duck into a side street
hoping for shelter and he found himself in a street full
of glass-fronted restaurants whose windows were silted
up with seafood. Angry-looking waiters touted business
in the streets. On a small bridge he came across a
woman, surrounded by suitcases, weeping. He thought a
lover or husband or parents had thrown her out and she
had nowhere to go. Everyone else hurried on, seeking
refuge from the rain, while he stood dripping and indecisive, afraid that like the husband of George Eliot, the
hideously ugly English novelist, she would fling herself
into the Grand Canal. 'What are you staring at, Arab?'
she yelled. 'Are you all right?' he spoke softly, hoping to
calm her. 'What do you think, shitball?' Now people
hovered, imagining that the coloured man was molesting
a white woman. Massoud felt like the Venetian criminals
of the Middle Ages, locked into cages suspended from
the campanile, left to starve or boil or freeze to death,
while the citizenry gathered to taunt them. He was
about to run when she rounded on him again. 'Goddam
taxi driver wanted eighty dollars so I have to haul all
this crap half way round the world and my fucking
arms are coming out.'

Deprived of the prospect of a public lynching the
crowds disconsolately shuffled on and the woman was
left to kick at her luggage. Massoud dived in and out of
streets, through laneways, over bridges, losing all sense
of direction until he found himself close to the Fenice
Theatre, where a girl in a pale pink suit paused in the
doorway. At first he thought he would walk up to her
and make conversation about the weather, which was

bad enough for discussion, but then he considered his
appearance, his streaming clothes. Young girls were
warned not to talk to strange men. He must wait until
he was in a suit and in a place of assembly. He paused at
a distance until she emerged and walked away, her plum-
pish bottom a bud on slender stems of legs, her red
umbrella a blown poppy. Her freshness burst upon his
mouth and limbs. Although he was pulled down by the
wetness of his clothing so that he resembled Venice's
imagined slaves, drowning in slime, he was almost
happy. He booked a ticket for that evening's perform-
ance of 'Samson et Dalila'. If she did not come, he
would return the next night and the next. After that he
hailed a taxi at the water's edge, paying its villainous
fare without a thought.

When she failed to appear he endured a brief panic,
seeking out the pink suit among the crowds. Then he sat
back, quite relieved, knowing from experience that happiness is nearest when just out of reach. The opera itself
came as a happy surprise. He had forgotten about music.
His time spent with the American girls had led him to
believe that all composition had degenerated to clashing
bin lids and angry bellowing.

The following day, which was Liberation Day, there
was a free concert of Verdi in the basilica. The air in the
basilica was thick with lust. Beneath the streaming,
crackling raincoats, fingers grasped. Eyes simmered
across banks of slender candles. Apart from people who
had come in to get out of the rain, the audience was
mainly Italian. Massoud did not have to bear the grief of
his isolation. He too was a worshipper, obsessed by the
woman in pink. He wanted to pursue her, to pay
homage to her. He wanted to tear away the mask of her
remoteness. In common with most worshippers his adora-
tion was without compassion. Like a butterfly collector

who pins his priceless find, his interest in her unusedness was to make its use his alone.

A recital in the music conservatory, which kept him dry in the afternoon, was a duller affair. A stout young woman thunked a harpsichord while Massoud gazed at a fresco of a naked goddess whose leg was laced to the knee with the thongs of her sandal.

By the evening he had developed a cold. He lay down on his bed at The Brooklyn, waiting for an aspirin to relieve his fever, but then his head began to ache and a burning set into his throat. His illness did not surprise him but he was astonished to have imagined that fate would allow him access to the object of his temptation. Sighing, he dismissed her, but when he closed his eyes to rest she was there, no more than a blush, demure and tantalizing.

'Go away,' he moaned. As a precious object in his household the minor illnesses of his childhood had been tented with circumspection by its army of females. He had retained an esteem for his adult indispositions which made the now-persistent image of his passion a matter of disrespect. He turned on his side and sulked. If he could clearly picture her face he would be content to ignore her but he had never seen her closely and was tormented by shifting images, trying to locate the perfect green for her eye, the daintiness of her teeth. After an exhausting hour's repose he flung himself out of bed, put on his silk shirt and hand-stitched suit and staggered snarling out into the rain.

He was late. When he got to the theatre the overture had begun and he had to stand until the interval. He waited behind a row of seats sniffing and inconsolable. Someone sitting in front of him turned and murmured in a low voice. 'No comprendo,' Massoud said without interest, having learned that it was Italians in Venice who listened to music. He sneezed as her warm body excreted a spew of heavy scent. He was about to move out of its range when she turned and spoke to him again. 'No com . . .' He stopped for he realized that she had been speaking to him in English and as his eyes became accustomed to the dark and he divined detail in its shadows, he acknowledged with an almost fatal shock, the leached pink of a suit, the glint of reddish gold. He leaned down close to her ear, risking her perfume. 'What did you say?'

She turned round fully this time and his heart contracted to the pip of a grape.

Her face, now mercilessly clear in the tamed gloom, was that of an angry Pekinese dog. She was about forty-five. Her hair had the scorched stiffness of repeated bleaching. 'I said,' she spoke in a bad-tempered Texan drawl, 'you bother me standing there.'

There was a moment, lighter than air, in which he thought death was going to relieve him, or even some rush of blood to the brain that would temporarily absolve him of consciousness, but then the moment passed and he had to walk away and find himself a seat, annoying several other people who hissed at him through their teeth. He slumped back, washed by fever and the after-waves of shock and humiliation while Delilah begged him to return her tenderness.

'Go away. I'll call the carbinieri!' Ellie Hewson yelped when she found the Arab following her after the opera.

'No, I only want to save you from the rain,' Massoud said with modest persistence. 'Tell me where you wish to go. I'll get a taxi.'

Ellie had often wanted to step into one of the water taxis that waited for the rich after the opera. She was tired of walking in the rain, of standing in a vaporetta, of counting out a little pile of notes and coins each night. A sudden gust of sodden wind left her exhausted and she allowed the small dark man to guide her into a comfortably covered boat.

'Where to?' he said.

'Harry's Bar.' She did not wish to admit, even to him, her lousy lodgings near the Rialto. She could afford a cappuccino if she walked back afterwards.

'Why Harry's Bar?' He remembered the toadlike woman eating asparagus.

'The Bellinis,' she recalled. 'They do real good Bellinis.'

When he stepped after her out of the boat and followed her into the restaurant, she shrugged in a mixture of rudeness and resignation. He bought her a Bellini and ordered fruit juice for himself.

She stared into the distance, her cross little muzzle a mask of dissatisfaction. He could tell she was embarrassed to be seen with him. Every so often she blinked with ire. Her green eyes were still beautiful.

At the opera, as the horror of their encounter subsided, he found himself trying to reconstruct his earlier impressions of her, to reconcile that crabbed countenance with the vision of grace he had composed inside his heart. He knew women. He was not a humorous or vivacious man but his talent lay in an absolute appreciation of the female essence. He had not imagined her composure, the delicacy of her solitude. There was something unformed about her that kept an aura of age at bay, so long as you didn't have to look at her too closely. The seductive music had soothed him and he observed that the singer was a stout and rather hairy-looking woman and yet she had the bearing of a beauty because she was the keeper of beauty. Was it the same with the dog-faced woman in pink? Was she the keeper of a secret? He reminisced upon the hovering blur of pink which he had first sighted, vulnerable and enticing. Curiosity possessed him and he began to be excited.

In his own country it was common to come upon girls of fifteen or seventeen with a beauty so intense that men almost went mad for them and their parents had to marry them off to keep them safe. By the time they were twenty-one the bloom began to fade and heaviness set in, but in the stout complacency of their maturity, they retained a leisurely acceptance of natural prerogative. It was different with the woman in pink. The matrons of his nostalgia carried a store of experience along with old vanity. Behind her ill-humour, the American woman still trembled.

Ellie Hewson was nineteen when she first came to Venice. She had no idea what she looked like except that she was too tall and hopeless at sports, and in the mirror of her companions she was a frizzy-haired, freckled, frumpish freak. She never had the right kind of jeans or sweatshirts. Her mother made her little tailored suits in cream or blue. She had spent her teenage years in an agony of pyjama parties and dances where no one spoke to her. She would endure her college years until she was old enough to find some dull, older man whose standards were not those of fashion. She would marry him and have kids and then nobody would notice her any more.

The visit to Venice was part of a student tour to Europe. She did not want to go, but her mother slapped down her savings so that Ellie could have the chances she herself had never had and worked like a maniac at the old Singer to give her a whole trousseau of little suits with gloves and sometimes even shoes to match.

By the time she got to Venice she had learned the knack of being alone. It was night-time when they arrived in deluge of rain. While the others were slinging strands of spaghetti at each other across the dinner table, she slipped away in her suit and headscarf. She found her way to St Mark's Square and went to Florian's.

She sipped at a brandy, making it last, admiring the delicacy of two young men until she became aware that they too were intently watching her. 'May we make a picture of you?' they said. 'I have no money.' She could not imagine what they wanted. They said they were students of drawing and wanted to sketch her. 'Why?' Ellie was cautious. 'Bella,' one of them explained, reaching out to touch her long, kinked red-blonde hair which five years later would become fashionable and would be called pre-Raphaelite, although few of its wearers would wonder why. Now it was just frizzy and a plague on her popularity.

'Bella!' men called out as she walked along with the other students who were fashionable in rag-ended jeans and sloppy joes. Soon she was removed from their teasing company. She was pursued by poets and painters, fêted by young waiters and rich old men. They admired the roundness of her face, her glowing skin, the budlike quality of her breasts. She was compared to a particular portrait by Bellini — some maddona, she supposed — whose luminous purity was no longer a feature of young girls. They even admired her mother's suits for Venice at its true heart is a formal city. The other students, they said, looked like gypsies.

A small smile moistened Ellie's dry red lips.

'What are you thinking?' Massoud disturbed her.

She turned on him distant eyes dappled with light and memory.

'When you look at me,' he said, 'your eyes go deep.'

The green eyes got a fossilized glint. She knocked back a second Bellini.

She had been taken to the opera, to small cafes where she drank red wine and ate anchovy sandwiches, to the Locanda Cipriani where she admired the red tulips rising out of a froth of forget-me-nots and ate an exquisite little green risotto and a plate of figs served on their leaves.

Dressed in her armour of flattery she developed a glow that made her the centre of attention, even among her own group. 'You're behaving like a tramp, Ellie Hewson,' the girl's told her. 'You'll end up with your strangled body dumped in the canal.' It would have suited her to end life on such a note although in a way life was now easier. For a time she became a celebrity. Girls tried to crinkle their own hair. Red-necked boys fought for her company having heard the fabulous rumours and believing they had to do with sex. In fact Ellie had kept her suit on through all of her Venetian encounters, not because she valued her virginity but she had so little experience even in the matter of flirtation that she thought she would make a show of herself in bed.

But she had been destroyed as well as created. When she went out with the boys back home, smelled their sweat and heard them talking about football and rock 'n' roll, she knew that she would as soon marry them as eat a skunk. Already she had begun to shrivel. Her moon face grew pinched with disapproval. She became a schoolteacher, which seemed like an escape, but in fact submitted herself to generation after generation of loathsome girls, all of whom had heard the legend of Venice but believed that she had invented it herself, and taunted her just as they had when she was their own age.

Massoud watched Ellie as she dreamed. He felt incalculably relieved that she did not want to talk about herself. She drank her Bellinis neatly and quietly, not even noticing when he replaced them and that she had now consumed four or five.

Studying her, he saw that the shrillness of her appearance was due in part to an unwise use of bright make-up and partly to the efforts of a country hairdresser who was trying to emulate a natural shade which she had described, inimitable. Her figure was still slender.

She had preserved herself, as near as possible, in the condition which once made her famous, clinging to the same neat pastel suits while they went in and out of fashion, endeavouring to paint on, as it faded, the glowing pallor of her skin, the incandescence of her burning fleece.

She had not been back to Venice until now. A quarter of a century was swallowed up by routine and duty and the aggravation of stuffing knowledge into teenage girls who were full of themselves. She lived on the promise that one day she would return. The young men would be middle-aged now, their beauty gone, but they had been sensitive and intelligent, with a love of music and paintings. She would come back for that and hope that they had made a little money, for she had none at all.

'All these years,' she said aloud, 'I've been living just to return. What do I find? Nothing! No one sees me. I'm left to carry my own suitcases, to eat my dinner alone. It's all vanished. Now what do I do?'

The Arab was more concerned than he need be, considering that he couldn't know what the hell she was talking about, considering she was roaring drunk.

'What are you looking for?' he said earnestly.

'Myself,' she wept.

He touched the dry skin of her face.

'Let me find you,' he begged.

Ellie didn't really know what she was doing. So she afterwards told herself. She was so drunk she could hardly stand. She needed to lean on him. All she could think of was bed: any bed.

When he woke in the morning, Massoud experienced a bright pang of triumphant joy. In the night, in the dark, all he could perceive were the features of her youth which time could not alter, the emerald eyes, the little snappy teeth and sharp red tongue. Her body was better than a girl's – ripe but firm; and it trembled. She was a virgin. So many lost years to be made up in a single night. So many continents in one small city. He had rarely known such beauty or such peace. Afterwards, watching her parted lips and once-used breasts, he felt he had experienced what he always dreamed of – a perfect marriage. He had known her as a girl, unwarmed and innocent, he had supplied her womanly greed, he had held her in his arms as she lay in the peace of death.

If only she would not wake.

When she awoke, Ellie looked down on Massoud's small brown shape in the blankets. 'My God!' she said.

For a moment they eyed each other gloomily but then he turned away, pretending to sleep while she flung on her garments and went downstairs to brave The Brooklyn's concierge's 'Buon giorno'.

When Massoud came out of the hotel the city had been transformed. It was washed clean. It sparkled with pure splendour. The water of the canal had been refreshed and returned the gaudy streetscape in impressionist relief. The sun was shining. For the first time since his arrival, it had stopped raining. Dazzled, he gazed around, his spirits soaring until he recognized a figure posed, graceful, against the bridge. It was Ellie. She was waiting for him.

'Good morning,' he said morosely.

'I want to show you something,' she told him.

He followed her to the Galleria dell' Accademia where she led him beneath the carved and gilded wooden ceiling, past three of four rooms hung with large paintings, dark and haunting. Her little heels clicked on the polished floor as she moved with confidence to a chamber of smaller paintings where she went directly to a painting by Giovanni Bellini of a young madonna with honey-coloured hair and lips as pristine as shells of coral. The girl was radiant. He was very moved.

To his dismay Ellie let out a yelp of laughter. 'Him and his damn cocktail!' she hooted. 'Do you know who that is in the picture? It's Mary Magdalen.'

Out in the street again Massoud attempted once more to take command. 'I would like to buy you a present,' he said.

A rancorous scowl touched the Texan's jaw but then she remembered with relief that she had lost her pride. 'I'd like a ride in a gondola,' she said.

'Do you want me to come with you?' he asked politely.

She shook her hed. 'I'd like to be on my own. Buy me a real long ride and I'll pretend I'm Lord Byron.'

When the boat sailed away she was standing up as Venetians do. The craft cut a silvery parting in the water, soft as a thrush's note. The sun put gold spokes into Ellie's dry blonde hair. He watched until the gondola gained its distance and was just a waxed black moustache on the flood of liquid marble, and Ellie some fairy creature, the merest shadow of gold and pink, fey in its hairy hold, insubstantial and unbearably lovely.

Walking in a dream he lost his way again and found himself on some quiet calle where an old lady shuffled along talking to herself.

'I have lost my ship,' she said.

She addressed the pavement. Like Massoud, she was monitoring her feet but it was not to protect her shoes from soiling, for she only wore old rubber sandals, but to keep an eye on the progress of her feet which gave no impression of toes and heels but seemed a sort of pincer formation.

Massoud was perturbed by her and trailed back and forth across the pavement echoing her; 'Your ship . . .'

When she heard English spoken she turned in gratitude, for she had been led to believe that she was in a foreign place, but then her ancient features fell bluntly into shock. 'Oh . . .!' She found herself looking at what looked like a saint in a suit, a lugubrious face in the olive tint so favoured in ikons, a golden tonsure of baldness.

'You're an Arab!'

'I am from Lebanon.'

She looked around as if for rescue and gave a noisy shudder inside her mac. 'What are you doing here?' She brought her glance back slowly.

The young man said nothing. To her annoyance she thought she saw tears come into his eyes but when she looked more closely he was smiling.

'I've lost my ship,' she reminded him, in case he thought he was the only one with problems.

When he walked away she clawed after him and in due course they found themselves on the Zattere where the cruise liner reared big and blank out of the small canal basin like a child's boat thrown in the lavatory.

'I've been on a cruise.' Now that she was safe the old lady wanted to talk. 'They put you off at different cities. You have to walk around until it's time to go.'

'Where did you visit?' he asked.

'I've been to Jerusalem. It was the moment of my life. I'm an Orthodox Jew. Now I'm going home,' she added with relief. She began to clamber up the gangplank, like an old crustacean scraping itself into the sand.

Scents of coffee sprang up from pavement cafes. Plumed vessels bobbed on water rejuvenated to a piercing blue. The sun warmed Massoud's head and he laughed as he strolled away towards terraces of palaces in biscuit and pink where feathery sprays of blossom hung over ornate balconies to dabble mauve fingers in the water, towards white-sheeted tables twinkling with lunch-time glasses, towards the breathtaking cacophany of genius and glitter and gawping spectators, walking and walking until it was time to go.

# You Don't Know You're Alive

Annie lived downstairs in the kitchen with the wireless and the Sacred Heart. It was a black sort of kitchen with a high, sooty wall outside the window and a long dark passage leading to the sink. The wooden draining board had developed a spongy texture at its edges, which attracted darting insects called silver fish and slow-moving beetles.

Gerald came home to his dinner at one and to tea at six. At noon, roused by the virginal clamour of two Angelus bells, Annie would put on her grey suit and red high heels and go down to the shops for some chops and when she got home she changed back into her jumper and skirt and put on the potatoes and got out the frying pan. When Gerald came in he turned on the wireless for the news. He ate in silence unless perturbed by something on his plate. 'What's this?' He would tap with his fork at some perfectly ordinary thing like liver. He seemed wary of food. He livened up when she put out his sweet and told her how much he dreaded his work. He was not suited to his employment, he said, and did not know how to face each day. She told him she sometimes missed work. It was quiet on her own in the house all day. She wouldn't mind if she had a sweet or a cigarette.

Gerald shook his head. 'You don't know you're alive. There's a war on out there.' He angled his glance towards a muddy scar on the grass outside that was called the birds' patch. Annie used to leave bread there for the birds so that she could watch them feeding but it became a stalking ground for predatory toms. When she found she had given herself a view of mangled sparrows, she threw any leftover bread in the bin.

Gerald drank a cup of tea after dinner, stirring in three spoons of sugar, and went back to work whistling. She left the wireless on for 'Listen with Mother' and 'Woman's Hour' and then she went upstairs and lay down, hurrying past the preserved dining room and drawing room, furnished with wedding gifts and never used. Gerald's complaints and the pitiful gaze of the Sacred Heart with His peeled-back chest wore her out. Sometimes in the afternoons she baked a tray of raspberry buns, using the sour pink jam that was reputed to be made from turnips or apples and tinted with cochineal, or she read a magazine which told her how to scrimp on soap and eggs and remodel a suit to save coupons. The medical pages were full of the secretive importance of mothers and babies and problems of a nature too personal to reply to in these pages and please send s.a.e. Sometimes she looked out the window at the wall and longed for a cigarette.

At four o'clock, when the light was beginning to fade and the smell of other people's fires was homely on the air, she put on her suit again and went out, walking as slowly as possible the quarter mile to the church where she lit a candle for a baby and lingered for a glimpse of Maevie Beatty.

Having nothing very interesting in her own life she pursued the adventures of this younger and more mature girl at an avid distance. Maevie had been coming to the church for more than two years. When she first appeared, bursting upon the dimness like a vision of Our Lady in pastel blue, she was Maevie Leddy from the post office,

giving thanks for her diamond engagement ring from
Billy Beatty. They were a lovely couple – Maevie round
and blonde and pretty and Billy tall and silent and
wolfish, a dairy farmer who was good to his widowed
mother. Maevie was nineteen then, with the kind of
glamour that appeals to both men and women. She
wore carmine lipstick and said she stuck to powder blue
because it brought up the colour of her eyes. There was
no sour edge to her conceit. When she showed Annie
her engagement ring, whispering in the painted shadows
of the long stained-glass windows of saints, she said she
never dreamed that such a thing would happen to her.
Annie responded fully to the excitement. It was an
event, when there were no longer any in her own life,
with the prospect that Maevie would soon be a married
woman like herself and then they could be friends.
Somehow Maevie outran her. She was quickly pregnant
after her wedding and became a gorgeous, overblown
rose. She made history in the village, giving birth to
triplets and got her picture in the paper, blowing out the
candles on her twenty-first birthday with three babies on
her knees. She was twenty-two now and pregnant again.
She was getting to look worn out. Billy's mother had
become an invalid and she had to look after her as well
as the three babies. Puffing around in the end of her
pregnancy, she had no time to bother about her hair and
clothes. All the same, Annie envied her just as she envied
Gerald in the office and the men out there getting killed
in the war. They were swept along by their lives.

On the way back she stopped at Fox's sweet shop and
Argosy Library and selected a paperback and sometimes
a comic, which she still liked. The evening air, buff and
foggy with the breath of coal, made her long for a
cigarette and she tried all the tobacconists, saying she
wanted five Woodbine for her husband, but they always

said the same thing, that cigarettes were saved for working men and her husband could have them if he asked
for them himself. She bought milk and bread at Carew's
and a half pound of small tomatoes which she ate from
the bag to give herself some sharp taste, arriving home
at the last possible minute so that the day would be used
up to when Gerald got home from the work that he
dreaded.

She lit the fire and changed back into her old clothes,
patting thick pink powder over her pale skin and a
lipstick in a red that was unrelated to any human tint,
that was like a hazard warning. While the rashers were
on the pan she fluffed up her hair. You could set your
clock by Gerald. The key was in the door as she filled the
teapot and she had the plates on the table when he came
into the kitchen and gave her her kiss.

He liked her red lips. They were his due. If she wasn't
wearing her lipstick, he would have asked her if she was
all right. He never kissed her ordinary young lips unless
they were in the dark. His look changed when she drew
them over with that dry red decor. It added an unnerving
edge to the evening as they read books or listened to the
wireless.

In bed she lay awake and thought about the girls; Joan
and Gladys and Kay and Rose. Before she got married
they were at the centre of each other's lives. Things that
happened only seemed real when they had picked over
them in the office. They ate bags of cakes and altered
one another's clothes and plucked each other's eyebrows.
Everything had to be done with one hand for the other
held a cigarette, smartly drooping. How smart they felt,
how hard-bitten, deftly pulling out and jamming in the
little black cylinders of the switch with two fingers
while ash fell from their cigarettes, telling Mr Hanafin
to mind his language, please sir, and reminding Mr

Arigho he was a married man. They worked for a lottery company that made its money selling tickets to America by mail order. Five hundred women took in orders and sent out tickets and were ambitiously pursued by the small staff of administrative males. They never minded anything the men did. Men were a separate species, like zebras or flamingoes. There were hunks and lechers and mickie dazzlers and good dancers and d.o.m.s, which stood for dirty old man. Good dancers and hunks were in demand but you had to have some sort of a fella because girls never had any money to go to the pictures by themselves. Annie was shocked when she learned that Kay 'went all the way' with men. It was unimaginable. It belonged in marriage. It was like learning lessons when you did not have to go to school. Kay said she couldn't stop herself. There were days on end when the red-headed country girl mooned around white in the face but then she would come screeching out of the toilet that her aunt had come and Joan would say the whole building could hear her and all the men were gone out to light a candle to St Jude, the patron saint of hopeless cases.

They all knew they would get married. It was an article of faith, a fulfilment of the years of straightening seams and ironing satin dresses and lying in steel curling pins. It was a diploma in their lives. The only time they were ever serious was when a fella asked one of the girls to marry him and then they would spend a whole morning, imagining his mother and what his children would look like, what he wore in bed – even if he was only a mickie dazzler.

Gerald wasn't a mickie dazzler. He was serious and had lovely manners. Annie said it was love at first sight, that she knew the moment she first set eyes on him. As far as the moment was concerned, it was the truth, but afterwards it was never the same.

The months of their courtship seemed endless. He kept her to himself and they were unable to chat in a comfortable way. The house he bought for her was big and already ageing. 'Solid,' was the word he used. She felt intimidated by it, as if she was back home with her mother and father. In spite of her doubts it was she who hastened the date of their marriage. It brought her closer to the girls again. 'Tell us what it's like, won't you?' they teased and she looked forward to meeting them afterwards as a married woman, to brightening her dark kitchen with their company.

She bought a hat for her wedding but Gladys said it was the wrong shape, it didn't suit her, and spent a morning in the office snipping it into pieces and sewing them back in an alternative form. She couldn't afford another hat so she had to wear it. The picture now hung in the hall of Gerald looking proud and Victorian and Annie, her eyes wide beneath the reconstructed hat which soared into a crooked peak like a tiled turret in a fairytale.

She never saw them again. She was a married woman. She hadn't any money to meet them for tea in Clery's or to go to the pictures. She had no telephone. She had taken for granted the luxury of her job on the switchboard. There was always some man making an excuse to ring her up, to call her little sweetheart. No matter what he said, or how sharply she had to answer back, she called him sir.

The first bomb was dropped on London the day Annie got married. Gerald often boasted about that, mentioning it to illustrate the indolent safety of her life. He wasn't criticizing her, but fondly affirming that he had given her a life of luxury. While she rested in the afternoons there were men in the trenches with their guts wrenched out. London city was a heap of rubble.

People ran through the streets in their nightwear as shops and monuments were consumed by flames. They huddled in the railway tunnels singing songs. Annie enjoyed these tales of adventure, although it didn't seem fair that none of it touched Ireland. To her it appeared that the people in the war had had a second chance, a reprieve from the lives they had made. Solid homes vanished in the night. Husbands were nobly dead. The women singing in the tunnels had got married and still they were free.

In bed Gerald sometimes told her of his childhood and how he had suffered at the hands of bullies or from jealousy of his brother. He talked of train journeys and chestnut trees. This astonished her. She had never dreamed there was anything to know about him. When she met him he was a good dancer and told corny jokes. She liked that. Now he was forcing her down some dark corridor that was nothing to do with the life she had agreed to share with him. One day, when she saw the girls, she would tell them, Gerald was a human being. Underneath the oiled hair and neat moustache and pristine suits in Prince of Wales check: a person. She would warn them. They weren't just fellas any more, after you married them.

The village where Annie lived was only three miles from the centre of Dublin but it still clung on to the country. There were two churches, a cinema, four pubs, a laundry and a bakery, but there were also farms close enough for the animals to walk to the abattoir that was in the village and Beatty's dairy farm down a lane behind a terrace of cottages. Children after school vanished into fields on the edge of the village. Faded green hills, neatly seamed, were stretched out on its horizon, like the eau-de-nil cardigans of aunts.

Twice a week Annie saw animals being driven to

slaughter. They picked their way along the edges of the road, past trams and cycles. Their look of anxiety made them seem like people. On Tuesdays cattle clattered through the gutters, fogging the air with their frightened breath and on Friday it was flocks of sheep. Annie always had to stand back and watch them. It upset her that although they knew what was going to happen, they did not protest, but only lamented.

One Friday, waiting for the sheep to pass, she made up her mind to step on the next tram and simply walk into the office and say hello. She had been married for two and a half years. Joan and Gladys and Kay and Rose might be married themselves, as they sooner or later must.

The air suddenly smelled sharp. She went into Carew's and bought herself some small tomatoes to eat. When she came out the Friday procession of sheep was still picking past its dainty path, bleating out an unhappiness that nobody minded. Annie wanted to let them know she felt for them. Absurdly she offered a tomato to a sheep. Even more foolish, it took it in its soft, luxurious lips. Annie patted its head and turned away but the sheep broke from its ranks and began to follow her. She tried to shoo it, even wasting another tomato by throwing it on the ground, but it was her the animal wanted. In a panic, because she hated responsibility, she jumped on to a tram, not bothering to check its destination. The sheep clambered after her. An old woman laughed at her; 'Mary had a little lamb,' and the animal shivered trustfully against her leg while a herdsman chased after the vehicle in the street. When the tram halted she had to lead the sheep off and hand it to the man who hit it with his stick. She did not want to go into town after that. She just bought the lamb chops for dinner and went home and waited until it was time to cook them.

The incident broke the final thread in some flimsy fabric that bound her to her past. Afterwards the office did not exist any more. It became a pageant of history with colourful episodes that played in her mind, unconnected to any real thing: the legendary parties with endless free drink that were once a year thrown for the staff by the lottery boss and which were plundered by hordes of gatecrashers.

Everyone came for the drink. 'I'm that thirsty, I could drink out of a po,' Kay used to say, her crooked blue eyes alight. The lottery boss had a mistress called Gerda Scully who was a dancer and he made her a present of a white poodle and a white sports car. It was said that any other man who looked at her was a dead man, even though he himself often tried to fondle Annie behind her switchboard. Once, after the party, Annie was driven home by Joe Finnegan, who was a famous lech but was very popular because he was a terrific dancer. 'Holy Malarkey,' he said, 'what's your mother doing letting you out in a dress like that?' She was indignant he should think her mother would have a say in what she wore. She made the dress because it was grown-up, a low-cut red satin worn with no bra. 'That's a bad girl's dress,' he said, when he stopped the car to kiss her. 'You're not a bad girl, Annie, are you?' The phrase pounded in her ears because when Joe Finnegan kissed her in her bad girl's dress she seemed to melt inside and flow soft and red as her red satin. Of course Joe Finnegan tried to go far and she had to slap him on the face. 'I'd give the sun, moon and stars for a night with you,' he said.

She would give the sun, moon and stars for one moment of excitement, for a cigarette. She could not believe that such an incident had taken place. She was more a woman now and more a child as well. She had a lovely body and had loved being unaware of it.

Now she dressed in women's clothes, making herself presentable for the neighbours. She was unconvinced by her married woman's uniform and it bothered her that others seemed to take it seriously. 'Good morning, missus,' the neighbours said when she went to the shops in her grey suit and gloves. They did not think she was an imposter. Was it the same, she wondered, for the soldiers in the war, taken away from all the important things in their lives – learning the latest dance steps and getting a date with a girl like Kay – plucked from tram stops and Sunday dinners and put in the mud of a foreign country, dressed up to kill?

Gerald had a cousin in the war. He was called Kevin and had signed up because he flew small planes for a hobby and wanted to be an airman. He was demobbed after his plane was shot down and now he was an invalid who had to be taken care of by his mother. He limped and had a scar. Gerald invited him to tea, although he did not usually like visitors. The scar on his face was a dark red with shiny unhealed bumps and looked as if someone had flung jam at him. Annie kept wanting to wipe it away. It was impossible to pretend to ignore it. 'Does it hurt?' she asked him.

'Children don't seem to notice it,' Kevin said, telling her that it hurt when a young woman made remarks.

Underneath the scar he looked like Gerald but Annie felt more at ease with him because he had given up the effort of manliness. All his stiffness had deserted him. She would have liked to talk to him. She wanted to say she was sorry she hurt him, and how he, without knowing it, had drawn attention to her disfigurement. When he spoke of children, it made her feel a failure for having no children who would sit on his knee and absolve his ugliness. She thought Kevin would have listened and understood but Gerald gave her a look and interrupted heartily: 'Drink, old man?' and he poured Kevin a giant whiskey.

Gerald blamed her for spoiling the evening for although he put on gramophone records and in spite of the whiskey, there was nothing more said. Kevin and Annie were marooned.

She had wanted to hear about the events that led up to Kevin's scar, to let him know he was lucky, that his was a scar of honour – not the honour of having fought for a cause because she did not understand about such things and suspected that he didn't either – but the honour of having lived through excitement. She was marked too, but by nothing. She had done nothing. Nothing bound and branded her.

If I had a baby, she used to think, watching Maevie Beatty struggling with a big pram, her stomach like a cabbage beneath a stained velour coat, we'd be a family. When she thought of a family she did not picture Gerald nor even the family she had grown up with, but something childish and carefree with games and picnics and a nice little face to look at while she walked to the shops.

She was not resigned to the intimacy of their double bed. As a child she had to share a bed with her sister and hated the touch of knees, the outflung arms or wandering strands of hair. Gerald startled her with his determination. 'He can't kill me,' she used to say, as when she was a child in school and the nun had found out she had done no homework. Soon there would be a baby and he would leave her alone.

When nothing happened she began to suspect she did not know very much. The girls talked about 'it' in work but they used code words which she only half understood. She knew that after you got married you stopped getting the curse and it meant you were pregnant. Her body went on just the same, indifferent to matronly imperative, a law unto itself. She could not talk to Gerald about such things. She attempted to discuss it with her mother but her mother in her absent-minded way said, 'You are not putting your mind to it.' It was true that she removed her mind as far as possible from the claustrophobic act of marriage, but every day she went to the church and lit a candle.

She waited there for Maevie Beatty and followed her out, trying to talk above the squall of three giant boys who pitched in their pram like bears in a fight. 'I'm trying to have a baby,' she told her. 'I've been married nearly three years.' 'I'm due next week,' Maevie said. 'It's twins.' She sighed. She seemed to have lost track of her concentration and even of her physical substance. She appeared as a vast, amoebic shape, in which her eyes were ghostly, enormous. Annie hung around, trying to inpress her. 'You don't know how lucky you are.' 'I have to get home,' Maevie said. 'Ma wets the bed these days.' Ma was Billy Beatty's invalid mother. Maevie gave a choking little chuckle. 'I'm twenty-three years of age and in a week's time I'll have six arses to wipe.' Annie was shocked by her coarseness and in awe of the fullness of her life.

A letter came. It was from Kay, to say that she was getting married. It did not bring the relief or excitement Annie would have expected. It had come too late. She put it in her pocket and kept it until Gerald went back to work after dinner. Kay was marrying a mickie dazzler called Bertie Gonagle. He was a little fellow with teeth missing. None of the girls liked him because he drank too much and became violent afterwards. She had to marry him, she explained, because she was twenty-nine. She would be thirty on her next birthday. Of course she did not tell Bertie Gonagle she was twenty-nine. She said she was twenty-four, which is what she told everyone else.

There was news of the other girls. Rose was married to a dote of a fella called Foley and had a little baby girl, Gladys (of all people) had got herself pregnant and could not even go to England on the boat because of The Emergency and Joan was still painting the town. Annie thought she ought to write to Kay but she knew she wouldn't. She couldn't congratulate her for marrying Bertie Gonagle and she couldn't try to stop her either, if she was twenty-nine.

Maevie Beatty vanished from the church to give birth to two more boys. Annie thought she was like a woman from the Wild West with her five sons. Her whole life was justified at the age of twenty-three. She would be surrounded by strength and admiration. She could do anything she liked now.

One evening, Kay dropped in on them after tea. They never had visitors. Annie was so startled she hid in the kitchen, leaving Gerald to cope. Kay swept down to the kitchen, which still had the dishes from the tea on the table, all glamour and a black eye. Annie and Gerald stood against the wall while she sat down beside the dishevelled table and crossed her legs and lit up a cigarette which she had got from God knows where. 'Go away, Gerry dear,' Kay blew smoke at him; 'and bring us back a big, big drink. I'm that thirsty I could drink out of a po.' To Annie's surprise Gerald did not give her a look but cracked a corny joke about pos and jerries, making a pun on his name.

Annie said: 'I haven't seen you for years.'

'It's different now.' Kay passed her a cigarette and lit another for herself and Annie at last felt relief. 'I'm a married woman now. We're in the same boat. Look at this!' She tapped at her black eye with a red polished fingernail. 'Gonagle did that to me. Only three weeks married and only half my size.' She sounded almost proud of his achievement. 'So, how are things with you?'

'All right,' Annie said.

Gerald brought them proper cocktails with a cherry on a stick and then when Kay told him to, he went away again. 'A real tame husband,' she said after he left the room. 'Aren't you the lucky one;' but, as when she had boasted of her own husband's violence, her voice now seemed tinged with contempt.

'Kay, I can't understand why I haven't got pregnant,' Annie said. 'It's nearly three years.'

'Count your blessings, kid, I say, but otherwise go and visit a doctor. What are they there for?' She left Annie three cigarettes and said she could get more any time she liked. She wrote down her address and made Annie promise to keep in touch, but when Annie went to see her after she had visited the doctor, Bertie Gonagle told her she was gone, she had run off with Willie Eccles who was a Protestant and played the piano in a band.

She had to tell someone her news, which stifled and startled her as if the doctor had announced that she was not a woman at all, but a mermaid. At first she had been harrowed by his pronouncement and protested that it could not be so. She felt ashamed. Was she always to be ashamed? The doctor said it was not altogether uncommon and a small procedure would put it to rights. In spite of his politeness it was so queer, it made her feel so alien, that she had to say it to some normal down-to-earth person or else she would live with the feeling that air did not touch her lungs like other people's, and her heart beat upon empty veins.

It would have been all right to tell Kay. Kay never minded about anything. It had to be someone who didn't care. Maevie Beatty had begun to return to the church and stood before the Blessed Sacrament shapeless and indifferent, her pram filled with new infants while the older ones worked their way loose from a push chair and prowled like incubi in the aisles.

She sat rehearsing the difficult words while Maevie stood and gazed at God and the children made havoc.

What could she be praying for now? She had a husband. She had a huge family, all of them healthy. What more could anyone want?

Maevie let out a cry and raised up her hands. The babies were cheered by this diversion but Annie wondered if she might be ill or in distress. She did not wish to be involved but forced herself to approach the young mother. 'Are you all right?' she whispered. 'Is there anything the matter?'

Maevie laughed right out loud. She turned around so that her upraised hand swung against Annie, hitting her on the head. 'She's gone mad,' Annie realized in sudden dread. She sat down quickly and Maevie, in a low voice, proceeded to abuse the tabernacle in a litany of foul language, unspeakable words cupped and flung back by the stone arches. An old priest crept out of the offertory and perched like a wind-swept seabird on the altar and then hopped away. The curtain of a confessional twitched and fell. Old ladies ceased their praying and looked up appalled to witness such foulness and such faith. Annie sat and shivered until in due course people hurried in from the street, strong men, a policeman and then Billy Beatty, and they pulled Maevie away. Some women gathered up the infants and wheeled them off in a different direction.

Maevie didn't notice. Her furious eye was still upon the altar. Her feet put up motiveless resistance as the men heaved at the bulk of her body.

When the church was quiet again Annie slipped into the confession box, where someone as cowardly as herself was hiding. 'I've been married three years,' she told the darkness, 'and I'm still a virgin.'

The doctor tied up her two legs while she went down into tunnels of disgrace as he peered into her body as no one had ever done, not Gerald, not herself. It was not allowed. She did not struggle as he tried to probe her and, ridiculous, told her to relax. Decently, he said nothing until she had put on her suspenders and stockings and the grey skirt of her suit.

When he gave her his verdict she gaped at him. 'But Gerald . . . It *hurts*,' she appealed. She turned her mind away when he spoke immodestly of things related to the inside of her body, of vaginal spasm and penetration and dilation. A little hospital procedure, he said, writing on a pad. She would be as right as rain.

When she had made her confession to the priest she felt ridiculous. She would never say such a thing to Gerald. She should have kept her secret. She got up quickly to leave but then the old man spoke to her.

'A celibate marriage is a very beautiful thing.' His dry voice was elated. She pictured it as dust dancing in a beam of sun. 'There is no greater gift for God. I should not have thought to hear of it in these modern times. God gives us all our chance for sacrifice, but few ever use it. God bless you. Your life is as fresh as the morning dew.'

Out on the street, she could feel it, in the winter dusk, the freshness of her life. It was still unused, still waiting to happen. Maevie Beatty's life was all expended but anything was possible for her, after a simple procedure. She was a bride again. She felt the years falling off, the clutter of nothingness blown away like dead leaves in a breeze. With the widows of the war, she had been given a second chance. She celebrated her happiness by walking home behind two women with prams, warming herself in the backdraught of their dull domestic chatter.

# The Picture House

My sister and I moved and circled like little flies in dusty light. Heavenly light came through the high lavatory window where exhausted rags of butterflies dangled in imitation of the stained-glass patterned paper that was peeling from the pane.

For a long time we did not meet any other children. We lived in a silent place. There was nothing to connect us to any species. We were each other.

We moved on instinct. When Lily put the pieces of a broken jam jar into her mouth to suck the jam it was I, a year younger, who crouched beside her and pushed out a long tongue. ''Mon Lily.' She responded to her mirror and I picked out the pieces, my tongue extended all the while. When the glass was gone and blood filled her mouth we both ran screaming to the mammy.

I was Matilda. We were planned as Lily and Tilly. Later, when I knew I had a face of my own and looked at it in a mirror I knew I was more of a Matty anyway.

When we were not moved by instinct, it was by stealth. Steal-th. The earliest wilful act I can remember was stealing snoke. Snoke was glucose powder, sweet and cold, which was kept in a blue and yellow box on the top shelf of the pantry. Snoke was meant for warm water and sickness but we preferred to lick it from a spoon. It became a craving. Sometimes I would wake violently at dawn to find Lily looking mournfully at me from her cot and we would creep downstairs in the foggy light of waking day. We climbed on a chair and wobbled there to reach the box. We dipped in our spoons and felt the cold white powder in our throats and drifting up our noses and soon we were comforted and could go back to bed.

Our thoughts ran together but we had our separate griefs. 'The nidle's on the roof!' Lily would cry when a huge moon, pockmarked and grinning, looked in our window. I was pursued by green and yellow girls who came out of the lavatory wall and laughed at me.

When we were four and five we fell in love. 'Are you my mammy?' Lily pursued the larger entity around whom our physical needs revolved and upon whom we had both become fixated with an unbearable crush. 'I am your mammy,' she agreed and we silently cheered.

Our father went away on business. Business was a terrible thing. Once he knocked on a farmhouse door and was pursued by a creature that was half a man and half a goat. He stayed in commercial hotels and locked the door to his room but was frequently wakened in the night by the dry squeak of its handle in the fingers of exploratory thieves. Sometimes, from these fearful excursions, he brought us back meringues.

When Father went away our mother turned the clocks to the wall and silenced the wireless. We piled into the double bed and curled up in the fleshy eiderdown. At odd hours of the day we would rise and do strange, elaborate tasks – scrubbing the red-tiled kitchen floor, washing sheets in a tin bath. Sometimes we went to the cinema or to church and when we were hungry we ate cheese sandwiches or chips. Most of the time we stayed in bed, watching a painting on the wall, which showed a purple mountain against grey skies while Mother told us stories of a life that was lived behind the magic mountain.

Her stories were about the girl who lived in a grey cottage on the far side of that hill, a girl who knew no obstacle, who tamed horses, mined gold, sailed rapids in boats of handmade bark. We did not know it then but it was in our mother's bed that Lily and I became different people. Her eyes lit up to the sound of horses' hooves, the splintering of a sailing craft in the teeth of jagged rocks. It was the stone cottage I loved. It had a log fire and copper pans on the wall. Yellow laburnum draped its poisonous charm over the roof and wild roses stifled the windows. The mountain itself, which protected the concealed cottage, had a fantastic property. It had no substance and the girl could ride through it and out of the picture, into the world. I preferred not to think about that.

One day I saw the house from the picture. Our Father had a car for his business and on Sundays after lunch he took us for a drive. The car had made a snorting ascent of a hill and as it floated silently down in a haze of dust and shimmer, the cottage folded back from the mossy shoulder of the slope. It was a perfect house, alone and empty, yet close to several cottages and a farm. Over another hill a grocery shop called Margaret Tuttle had its name picked out in blue and gold.

Around this time we found out about death. A cat had been discovered in the garden, its stiff paws neatly folded. Our parents patiently and confusingly explained mortality. The cat was dead as all God's creatures must die and no one ever knew when. You went when you were called. You could not hide as you hid when your mother and father called, for God saw all things.

'If we die can we all go to heaven holding hands?' I asked our mother but she smiled and said no, she and Daddy would die long before we did.

I did not trust them after that. They would go when

God called them. We would be left behind. I began to prepare for death. When we had money I would not spend it nor let Lily spend hers but hid it beneath the wing of a cloth duck.

It happened when I was almost six and Lily was seven. Mother was sick and went to the doctor. She was sent to the hospital for tests. That was the end. We knew because Father would not let us see her. 'No children allowed!' he said, but that was foolish for sick children live in hospital.

After two weeks we asked one another:

'Where has she really gone?'

'She has gone to death,' I said.

'Dead!' We thought of the hairy coldness of the cat. Lily's face trembled and I patted her cheeks.

Father had to go away on business. 'Now what will I do with you two?' He looked as if we were an inconvenience, left over from better times. 'I suppose it is time you went to school.' His face had a blue and wobbly look like an egg that is not properly boiled. He would not look at us. I knew that he was going to go away and would never come back, that he would not think of us again unless he passed a baker's window and glimpsed meringues.

Our world was being pulled away from us. We were like the birds that lived in the hedges and then the men cut down the hedges and the birds balanced, quaking, on thin air while eggs seeped into the ditches and in the grass the crinkly necks of nestlings rose in lonely answer to their mothers' cries.

We ran away. I packed all the things we would need. We went in the night when Father was in bed, creeping down the stairs as quietly as if we were only coming down for snoke.

Things look different at night. Even our own street

was stretched out of shape with shadows. We had never been out this late before. We had hardly been anywhere on our own. The cases were pulling our arms off. 'Let's go back, Matty,' Lily whined. 'We'll run away in the morning.' I told her no, we must learn to stand on our own two feet. Father used to say that when we asked him or Mammy to do little jobs for us, to button our coats or put sugar on our bread. By now I was used to telling Lily what to do. Secretly I thought she was right and hoped that someone might see us and take us back. A man coming out of a public house in the village laughed at us. 'Gremlins! Where do ye think you're going at this hour?' He gave us such a fright that we ran all the way home, bumping the cases off the ground, afraid of his big yellow face, afraid of gremlins.

When we got to the house we were reluctant to knock on the door, fearful of waking Father, but I had forgotten to close the door so we pushed it gently and tiptoed in. Lily turned a yawning face to me and smiled and sighed with gratitude.

'Tomorrow,' I told her severely; 'first thing.'

We went to bed and fell asleep and were woken in the morning by Father who was cross and puzzled to find us beneath the blankets with our overcoats and our shoes and socks on.

During the day, when he was at work, a woman came and looked after us. One day she was late and Father had to leave before she arrived. After we had sat for a while with our breakfast I looked at Lily and nodded and her blue eyes flared up with excitement and fright and we got our coats and our cases.

We went on the bus. The cottage was up a road near a church which was past the village next to ours and we told the bus man to let us off at the church. He lifted us down from the platform and handed us our cases and he said: 'Your mammy should be ashamed.' 'We have no mammy,' Lily said. 'Our mammy is in heaven.' The man was thin and white inside his navy uniform. He had a bump on his neck which rose and fell. He looked at us and got tears in his eyes and forgot to punch the bell.

When we reached the cottage I got a fright. This was the first time I had seen it close. It looked awful. The windows were gone and nettles crowded out, waving their dusty teeth.

'Home,' I said doubtfully to Lily. 'Don't be afraid.'

'I'm not afraid.' She spoke through her nose, which was gripped in her fingers. 'I'm hungry. There's a smell.'

'Farmyard beasts,' I laughed. 'Sheep's heaps.' But I was very nervous. I thought now that we ought to go home or to school or wherever there were windows and beds. I saw then, hidden beneath the weeds and grasses, a path. It was made of tiles in different colours to form a pattern. A lot of the tiles were broken but you could still see how it was meant to be and how it must have pleased the people who had come to the cottage once upon a time, when it was new. 'Look, Lily! It's a real house. Look at the path!'

'It's not a real house!' She too had made a discovery. 'There's no toilet!'

It was my house. I would look after Lily here. We didn't have to trust anyone else, grown-ups who would die or go away on business. We had each other and Mammy had said that we would not die for a long, long time.

'Now, Lily;' I took my sister by the arm. 'We must pretend this is a doll's house and that we are the dolls. I will tidy our house and you will make our dinner.'

'There's no food!'

'Well, of course there is food.' I sounded like our mammy now and Lily heaved a sigh.

'In here, look!' I opened the case I had been carrying. At home, over several days, I had taken from the pantry all the things we liked; cornflakes and cream crackers and Marmite, packets of jelly and Mandeville cheese, apples and sugar and drinking chocolate and snoke. 'We won't know ourselves.'

'What's in the other case?' She pointed like a policeman.

'Everything,' I said proudly. 'Bowls and cups and spoons, a knife, a candle, matches, our quilt, socks, my cloth duck.' I had given a great deal of thought to our packing.

Lily stood like a princess, imperious, unwilling to be pleased. 'What about soap and a facecloth and comb? What about my nightie and my teddy?'

'We have put all that behind us now.' I did not want to admit that I had forgotten such important things. 'We must learn to make do with little, like the savages.'

'I don't want to be a savage,' Lily cried savagely. Her knees shook as they always did when she was excited and about to cry.

'Din-din,' I wheedled. 'We can have cornflakes.'

I went into the cottage, pulling my sleeves down over my hands, to cut the nettles. 'There's no milk!' I heard Lily's mournful discovery but I took no notice for, as I cut away the weeds with the steel bread knife I had brought, I saw that there was a part of a stone floor remaining and a fireplace which must still work because there were ashes and bits of burnt stuff in it. I was entranced to think that real people had been in the cottage and that they had used it, not for play, but for real life. It was like seeing Santa Claus.

When I had cut down the nettles I got the quilt and folded it on the stone floor. Then we sat outside and ate dry cornflakes and cream crackers and sucked on some jelly cubes.

We made daisy chains and counted distant cows. We dared each other to climb the hill behind the cottage to see if you could walk through it but we were too tired and uncertain of ourselves. We played 'I spy', watching the village below the fields and then we lay on our backs to look at birds in the sky and soon we fell asleep.

Wc woke to hot afternoon sun and thirst. We had to have milk. 'What will we do?' Lily moaned. I had money. I was very proud of this. 'We'll go to the shops like our mammy used to do,' I said.

'And whose little girls are ye?' Margaret Tuttle said when we asked her for milk and bread and a quarter pound of corned beef.

I touched Lily's hand and whispered. 'Don't say anything. Our mother told us to hurry,' I said to the woman whose teeth clanked in her smiling mouth.

'Are ye new here?' She put a bottle of milk on the counter.

'We're on our holidays,' I lied.

'Where so?' With a big knife she cut slabs from the block of pressed meat.

'In an old, mouldy, falling-down cottage!' Lily said suddenly, as if woken from sleep. 'Filthy, horrible!' she cried with vehemence.

'The cut of you!' The woman suddenly observed, her knife raised in the air in alarm. 'Where's your mammy?'

'We have no mammy,' Lily said.

'We have to go now.' I reached for Lily's hand. 'Our father's waiting for us. In a car.'

Margaret Tuttle's head reared like a horse's, out the window and around each visible twist in the valley. I grabbed the milk from the counter and we ran.

'Why did you do it?' I pushed and pinched Lily.

'Because I want to go *home*!'

'There's no one there. They've all gone. If you don't let me look after you, no one will.'

'I don't care, I hate you. You're a liar and a thief!' Her voice was high and thin and hopeless.

It was all because she had to go to the toilet. She always hated having to go in strange places, having to *say*. When I said that she must go behind a tree, must use leaves and grass, her bottom lip folded down and her eyes bulged at me as if I was a boogie man.

I brought daisies from the field into the cottage and put them in a cup. I got sticks and twigs and laid them in the grate to make a fire. I had matches. I had watched our mother light the fire.

It would not catch flame. At first when I held the match to the sticks a little grey thread of smoke appeared. I put a pile of matches in the fire and held a lighted one to them. There was a big flash and a lot of smoke.

I had sometimes seen our mammy hold a sheet of newspaper across the grate when the fire was slow. There was no newspaper. When Lily came back I made her take off her slip and hold it up. A golden light bloomed behind this gauzy screen. We watched, mesmerized as the flames pranced and then very slowly a bright yellow frill of it escaped out of the grate and clung to the bottom of the slip; then waves of it climbing, climbing eating up the white cloth, leaving a crisp, black smelly wafer dangling below.

Lily danced out into the room.

'Let it go. Let it go. 'Mon, Lily,' I said in a quiet voice.

A burst of orange leaped up and took the froth of hair at her forehead, turning golden curls into blackened cuphooks. Lily clamped her hands to her head and screamed. The slip writhed up towards the ceiling, waving and trembling like a magic carpet. In a while black snow came down, black as the sticks in the grate where the fire had once more gone out.

I made a party to cheer us up, cubes of jelly and apples and a paste from drinking chocolate and milk to spread on cream crackers. Lily cried as she ate and chocolatey spit ran out of her mouth, down her chin and over her dress. It didn't matter for we were both black from the smoke of the fire.

I put her to bed. 'Wait here,' I said. I went and got the glucose powder and a spoon. 'Eat as much as you like.'

'How long will we stay?' Her breath was still shaky from tears and it blew a storm of white grains around her mouth.

'For ever,' I said.

'What about our daddy?'

'He's gone away. Gone to business. He's never coming back.'

'What about my husband? When I grow up I have to have a husband.'

'We'll see.' I took the snoke away and wrapped the quilt around her. Poor Lily looked an awful mess. I thought she would not last very long, that she would start to die like our mother in a little while. I was as strong as a horse. I got the candle and lit it and walked around the cottage. 'This is my house and I am its owner,' I said. Then I went to bed with the cloth duck. Before I lay down I prised beneath its wing. A shower of silver came out, like water from a duck's wing; three pounds and ten shillings.

In the night the real owners of the cottage came; spiders big as spools of thread and slugs that oozed out between the stones. I listened to mice or rats scratching at our case for food. It was a careful sound like tearing or sweeping. I heard a cry and put an arm out to comfort Lily but Lily was sleeping. The cry had been mine.

Lily woke first in the morning. Her eyes and her skin looked red and terrible. 'Milk,' she said in a scratchy voice.

We had none left from yesterday. We could not go back to Margaret Tuttle. By now she would have told on us. Someone might be searching for us.

'There are houses over the hill,' I said. 'I will ask there.'

'Don't leave me alone,' Lily wearily pleaded.

'All right then. You can come.' I would have preferred to go alone for if anyone was looking for us it was two girls they sought, two girls with long hair. 'But we'll have to make a little change.' I took the knife I had used for cutting the nettles and seized Lily's hair. 'Nooo!' She put her hands over her ears, although the noise the knife made was just a small, dry sound, quieter than mice or rats. It only took a minute. I held in my hand a big bunch of her cloudy hair. The hair that was left on her head looked like a drawing filled in by numbers.

I was glad Lily could not see herself and hoped my hair looked better when I had forced my sobbing sister to saw round its edges. We went out, carrying our cups. We were both shivering for it had been damp in the cottage all night. We headed for the nearest house and beat upon its door.

A man answered. We looked hopefully around his bulk, thinking there must be a woman deep inside the house but there was only a girl, not much bigger than ourselves, who hid behind her father. We were both unsure of men and this one wore his underwear.

'Milk, please.' I held out my cup.

'Ragamuffins,' the man commented without interest. 'Would you like to see my rabbits?'

I nodded, deeply ashamed that he had called us untidy.

He gave us cups of milk and showed us wooden cages in his garden, from which white rabbits peered out with their pink eyes. All the time he was followed by the girl who had white hair and pink eyes and who peeped at us from behind him. He said he had bantam hens too but we were both afraid of the rabbit girl and we quickly left when the milk was finished.

The cottage looked safe as we came back to it. I thought it seemed more homely this morning. It looked different but I could not think why until Lily pointed. 'Smoke!'

It came from the chimney, a fat brown curl. Someone had lit a fire. Someone was in our cottage. I broke into a run.

'Oh, no, Matty!' Lily begged, but she ran after me.

It was a dirty tramp. He had lit a huge fire and for a moment this held us and we stood in the doorway and stared at it for it had begun to rain and we were very cold. 'This is our house,' I said then. 'You go away or I'm telling on you.'

He turned angrily but when he saw us he gave a stupid sort of laugh. 'You tell on me and I'll tell on you.'

He turned again to the fire. He was gulping a bottle of sherry wine.

'You should go now,' I said. 'Our father is coming.'

He stood and gazed beyond us to the drizzly field. He looked wild. When he saw that there was no one he gave another laugh, turned once more to the fire and fell with a thump like an apple from a tree. The dregs of the wine trickled into the mud.

For a while we stayed where we were with streams of wet running inside our collars.

'Is he dead?' Lily said.

Oh, no. He was not dead. A torrent of snores sputtered out of his growling face. Soon he would wake and he would tell on us. I went into the cottage and stood by the fire watching him. Steam puffed out of my clothes. He looked awfully hard, the man, but all the same I got the knife and held it up as high as I could and then closed tight my eyes and drove it down and pushed and pushed. I did not look at him but when I opened my eyes again Lily was looking, her eyes huge, her face growing longer and whiter. She came forward with mincing steps, as in a ballet, then moved slowly sideways and lowered her head like a swan and was sick all over the quilt.

We went home after that. We did not know what to do with the man and we could not sleep on a quilt full of sick.

'My God! My God!' our father said, when we walked into the house. He bent to hold us but his face was full of fear and it frightened us and made us cry. 'We thought you were dead,' he said. 'There were dogs out looking for you.'

We were washed and given soup and put to bed – our own bed with our teddies – and then Father asked if there was anything else we wanted. 'Mammy!' Lily sobbed sleepily.

'Yes,' our father said; 'yes. She is getting better. She has been so worried about you that I think we can bend the rules. You will both see her tomorrow.'

We slept all day. In a little while Mother came home from hospital but nothing was ever the same again. Lily had changed. She was no longer mine, no longer beautiful. She kept her hair short and her face stayed long and white as in the moment when the knife fell. Afterwards

I asked and asked: What did the man look like? Where did the knife hit him? Was he bleeding? Was he dead? 'I can't remember,' Lily would say in a daze.

I was different too. Perhaps I had the power of death and although I would never know I thought I would never forget. Always, I thought, I would see him, blood growing like an ornament on his head or on his chest, a look of terror in his open eyes like the look on the face of God who sees all things, who is all-powerful, except in His powerlessness not to look.

After all, it was not the man I remembered. Sometimes I even found it hard to remember the pattern of tiles outside the cottage. Mother no longer told us stories of the magic mountain. She was often tired and liked to rest alone. 'You are big girls now,' she would say with relief. Lily went away to school but I stayed home another year. I was left with time on my hands. I ate a lot, for I had been hungry in the cottage, and waited to see what would come into my mind.

It was the dogs. It was that one moment when our father held us close to him and then gave us the astonishing news that they had sent out dogs to look for us.

Why had they not come themselves?

When I asked him he said that these were very special dogs. They were called tracker dogs and they were trained to follow your scent.

We had no scent. Our mother had a scent called *French Fern*. She hardly ever wore it but sometimes took out the stopper and let us sniff its deep green smell.

I saw the dogs, bounding over fields and hills, past the farm with the white rabbits and the rabbit girl, past Margaret Tuttle, her big clanky mouth full of secrets unreceived. They would come to the cottage and take great alarmed breaths of its past life, of smoke and sick and maybe some old skeleton smell. Soon they would raise their noses to fresher and more appealing scents, wild rabbits and sheep and squirrels. Who would set out to search for them when they grew thin and wild?

I saw them drooping in summer heat; searching old tins and drains for water, or huddled together in the snows of winter, moaning softly in their sleep as starvation came closer, scratching slow as a rat. I saw them rise in the grey and hungry morning, blink softly at some distant memory of home, then shake themselves wearily and totter off, sniffing the ground and the air, searching, searching, searching, for two girls who would never come back.

# *Affairs in Order*

---

'Jocelyn's dying,' Rose said to Angela when they met for tea.

The effect on the other middle-aged woman was as if the pink cake she was sectioning had suddenly shown beads of blood on its sawed edges. She did not seem surprised nor saddened but utterly run through with horror.

'Jocelyn?' Her face went white and her eyes were helpless and dreadful.

Rose had been through all this the week before and was able to eat her cake. 'He's been given a month – five weeks at the most.'

'Jocelyn . . . oh!' Angela moaned. She dropped her gaze, and found no comfort in a view of her caged bust. 'Is he in hospital?'

'No,' Rose admitted with regret. 'Martha seemed determined to keep him at home.'

Jocelyn Fowler had known many women in his youth. He had a profound effect on all of them. One later went mad and another entered a convent. Those who afterwards married, or who remained married, stayed in love with him all their lives. Their husbands had something to thank him for, for they never looked at another man.

He was a poet, and with the hair for it. In the plain stretches of life, women particularly remembered the buttery feel of his heavy gold hair.

He wasn't especially a sexual man. He was full of conversation and fun, watching his women with blue, interested eyes, waving his long arms and folding long legs. Sex was an interlude or an accompaniment. He made love to his girls as a man at dinner eats from the fruit bowl during intent debate, but afterwards he always wrote so tenderly about their private parts.

His marriage to Martha was a surprise – Jocelyn, tall and graceful, with the golden (now silver) flow of his curls; Martha, squat as a letter box, with her cottage-loaf bosom and brown and grey crewcut. Some said she had money. Others assumed that he had grown serious and that she was to be the custodian of some epic work. In the first year he produced with great flourish (and success) a small volume of verse about housewives in Sainsbury's and cats watching 'Coronation Street'. After that there was nothing but an introduction to a book of photographs and an endorsement for a wristwatch. People blamed Martha. She had dulled him. She had swallowed his soul.

When Martha answered the door to Angela, her wholesome face was scarcely altered by grief. She seemed distrait, but not swollen by weeping. She had an air of irritation.

'Oh, Martha! Oh, my dear!' said Angela, who looked a wreck.

'Hello, Angela.'

'It's been so long,' Angela said; 'and now this awful news. How is he?'

'Jocelyn's dying.' There was something strange about her, standing there with her dull blue dress and her bristly hair. She seemed like a child, ill-mannered and feckless, unable to take in the stretch of death. She wasn't even looking at Angela.

It was the shoes. Her gaze had been distracted by the

extraordinary height of the other woman's heels. The older women all wore high heels. They took great pains to effect youth in their faces but age crept back in the discomfort of their footwear. The young girls wore any old thing – runners or wellingtons or mountaineering boots. Legs did not seem a feature of the whole business any more. Martha could never think of anything to say to women like Angela. She knew that they discounted her. She had been plain when they had been beautiful. They attached great potency to the past and seemed not to have noticed that they were all getting on anyway when Jocelyn married her and none of them looked all that much better or worse than the other: except Joss.

'Come in, Angela,' she frowned. 'Say hello to him. I'll put the kettle on. He's very weak. Try not to stay longer than it takes the kettle to boil.'

Inside, Angela peered around briefly, surprised by how comfortable the house was, the attention that had been given to flowers and lace and polish. Martha pointedly filled the kettle and Angela fled quite nimbly up the stairs. She found Jocelyn in a bright room in a feathery bed by a window. Most of the flesh was gone from his face and there were lines of suffering on his delicate skin. His hair had been saved and had taken on the quality of rolling clouds. His blue eyes were huge and full of vision. He looked magnificent.

'It's me,' she said shyly. 'How are you dear?'

The look he gave her was kind and full of suffering. Love bubbled to her lips and her eyes dissolved. He stretched out his hand. 'I've been summoned,' he wryly smiled.

'Oh no.' She took his fingers and pressed them to her mouth. 'You're running out on us. You're escaping, leaving the rest of us to grow old and lonely alone.'

'Don't cry, sweetie.' He brushed her cheek with a

leaf-dry thumb. 'I've had a good life.' His use of past tense refreshed her sense of terror. 'I've never stopped loving you,' she said.

'Come here, girl.' He put out his two arms and drew her frailly to his chest. She allowed herself to go with him until she was lying against him on the bed, her mouth on his hair, her flesh on his flesh, just as it used to be, apart from the blankets and corsetry that now divided them.

She did not rest her weight against him, for it was more substantial than it used to be, and his was less, but allowed her body to learn again the geography of his bones. In a while, mad memory was awaiting his mouth, which used to turn from energetic talk to find her lips, and kiss. Then he would swing her body underneath his to admire it and then kiss it here and there and then he would make it his home.

He seemed so relaxed against her, so peaceful. Nothing changes, she told herself, except the circumstances of happiness.

After a short duration of this relative bliss Angela heard, in her mind's ear, the furious boiling of a kettle. She sat up guiltily, disturbing Jocelyn, who was almost asleep. When she went into the bathroom to mop her eyes, she was surprised by her wild, tousled look.

At the bottom of the stairs, as she descended, there stood a strange woman. 'Where's Martha?' Angela said. The woman gave her an angry look and swept past her in the direction of Jocelyn. Some sort of aria was going on on the front step – the sound of a young person thwarted and Martha's responses, soft, but not in the least yielding: 'No, I'm afraid not – he's very ill. You can leave a message if you like.'

'An old friend of Jocelyn's,' she explained to Angela, when she had managed to lock her out.

'Not old, by the sound of it,' Angela said.

'No, actually.'

'Poor you,' Angela sympathized. 'So many people to tell.'

'I told no one,' Martha said. 'It was Joss.'

Martha's behind, as she wandered back to the kitchen, resembled one of those family joints of meat that are tied about with string. Angela suddenly thought she understood. The past was not past at all. Jocelyn's life awaited resolution. He had to put his affairs in order. She followed Martha, stalking like a mud-dwelling bird on her aerial heels.

'Let me help you!'

'Yes, get the milk jug.'

'With Jocelyn! You must be worn out. I could come and sit with him. I could sit nights if you like. I'm a widow now.'

'Jocelyn doesn't need anyone to sit with him. He needs sleep. I like to read a little to him in the evenings, but by the time all the visitors have left, he's too worn out.' She looked forlorn, suddenly, like an old tree on a blasted heath. 'Did you know Baba Maxwell?'

'Who?'

'I think she's Mrs Something now. The woman in the hall! He was in love with her once. He told me. He wrote that very peculiar series of poems about her — "Flowers in the Night".'

They were about me! Angela thought with a pang of jealous fury. Jocelyn had read the poems aloud to her in bed. She was young then, and almost innocent. It was a seduction like none other, to be teased with your own body: well, to all intents, your own body. He had employed, as poets do, poetic licence. He depicted a flower, 'with peeping scarlet stamen, winning as a kitten's tongue'. She herself had a very reclusive physiognomy.

The thought of that woman with her scarlet stamen sitting up there with Jocelyn – possibly even lying on his chest – agitated Angela beyond endurance. She could not stay in his house.

'Aren't you going to have your tea?' Martha pondered. Angela said no. A new grief slopped about in her chest. Martha too seemed to have lost heart and stood nursing the teapot with its inch of warming water.

When the visitors first began to arrive she assumed that it had to do with publishing. No publishers came. There wasn't any new work and the old had already been recycled. Had the literary world mourned the death of the poet years and years ago? Had she yielded her life to a gorgeous man? Who was she, in any case, to quibble? Other women seemed to think the latter more than good enough for her.

They came in cars, on buses, by motorbike. Their perfumes fled about the house, their grapes and freesias proliferated and went mouldy. They were used and unused women, successful and failed ones, young and old. There were women with glorious hair, with hairs on their chin, with gold in their teeth, with emeralds sunk into beds of metal, biting plump, waxy fingers.

There was even a nun. She was unique. At first she seemed incredibly old. She was wrinkled and shrunken and had a crone's shambling gait. It was only when she looked up and one saw those vivid eyes that one knew she was woman in her prime. She had merely tipped over from rosiness to an intense withering, like an apple stored in the light.

She, of course, did not wear high heels. Beneath the coarse wool of her robes, her horny toes were splayed in sandals. She carried a large black bag made of imitation leather.

'Soeur Gertrude,' she introduced herself to Martha.

She offered no such relief to Jocelyn but slithered straight up to his bed and stared at him with her bright blue eyes. 'Bonjour Jocelyn.'

He kept his sheets clutched to his chin and scowled at her to deter her. What was Martha thinking of? A terrible notion struck him then, borne on the intense beam of her gaze. He managed to pull himself up a little bit to study her. 'Gertrude?' He gave a gasp of recognition and she a small smile, rather cruel.

'Gertie?' he said. 'Gertie Balfour?'

Soeur Gertrude did not fling herself upon his chest as other women had done. Instead she placed upon it numerous small portions of the corpses of saints, taken with care from her black bag. Then she prayed. He watched the dried fruit of her lips, the rapturous fluttering of her brown lids.

She was the most beautiful of all the girls he had known. For a year he had pursued her, trying to make her say she loved him. When he succeeded, he was frightened by the ferocity of her commitment and he had violently shaken her off. There followed a silence so complete that he imagined she must have died but he found out from friends that she had entered a convent – a contemplative order where the sisters spoke rarely, and only in French.

She finished her prayers and gathered up the relics and put them back in her bag.

'Will I get better now?' Jocelyn jested.

'Si Dieu le veut,' she replied.

He found her more interesting than any of the other women and curiously, less changed. She had the same directness of manner, the same seething air she had had as a girl. Whereas the other women were softly spoiling, she had simply cast off what she no longer needed when she gave herself to God. He was intrigued now, as when he had first met her, by her apparent lack of interest in him. 'Gertie, Gertie,' he said in humblest tones. 'I treated you badly.'

She peered at him rather rudely, as if trying to recollect what he was talking about. 'You were a stage on a journey,' she commented at last. 'Journeys are seldom comfortable.'

'Have you heard the news about Jocelyn?' Rose said to Angela, when they met for more tea.

'Has he croaked?' Angela said brutally.

'No, actually. It's rather the most extraordinary thing. He's begun to get better. They say he's had a remission. It's a miracle, really.'

Angela contemplated her cake. She cut it up and then returned to the pastry any jam and cream that still adhered to the knife. Four quarters of a cream slice were consumed with intent and the debris deftly sifted from her lips with a napkin. When the napkin came away, the lips retained their expert coating of lacquer. There also remained behind a look of disgruntlement which was new, but seemed chiselled in at the edges.

'I wonder,' said Angela, 'if he ever really had cancer at all. I shouldn't be surprised if he made the whole thing up to get attention. He always was a bit of a fraud.'

'I know that,' Rose said sharply. 'I didn't know you knew.'

Now that he was getting better Jocelyn would have welcomed visitors. He would have eaten the fruit and drunk champagne and had a bit of music in the background. Oddly, they seemed all to have vanished. It should have been a festive thing, turning back at death's door, but he was left alone, as if in disgrace.

Now, he needed people. Dying had been an absorbing business but recovery was filled with hindrance and frustration. The absence of pain left an odd hollowness in his life. He could not yet quite do things for himself and Martha was never there when he needed her.

What on earth had happened to Martha? She seemed to have missed the news of his recovery. She trailed about in a grieving daze, eyes bulging with depression. When he summoned her she would come reluctantly and look at him as if he was an interloping stranger.

This morning she had forgotten lunch and he had to ring the little bell she left with him. When she came, she bore no tray of soup and fruit, nor apologized for its absence. He could not ask. He was at her mercy. He smiled his most winning smile.

'I'm going back to work, Joss,' was all she said.

'What can you do?' He spoke rudely out of fright.

'I can do a lot of things.' She faced him quite squarely. 'I was working when we met.'

He stayed quiet a moment, letting the steam go out of his anger. He patted the velvet-covered stool beside his bed and she allowed her bottom to subside on to it. 'This is absurd, Mattie. I'm an old nuisance, I know, but I still need someone.'

'I've arranged for a nurse,' she said. 'I'll be home in the evenings.'

'What am I supposed to do all day?'

The same as me. Go back to work, she thought. She did not say it. She shrugged. He understood that she could not be bothered to discuss it. As soon as she decently could, she got up to leave.

'Is it the old girls?' he called out fretfully. 'Is that it?'

'What?' she turned at the door.

'Something's changed. Aren't you glad I pulled through?'

'Leave it, dear.' She went out quickly. How foolish she would feel if he forced her to tell the truth.

It was his unreliability. Over the years she had put up with him because she understood that they would be together when they were old. Now she felt betrayed. He had shown her that he did not need her. He could turn away without a backward glance and drop out of her life.

She went into the garden and sat sunning herself on a wooden seat over paving stones whose seams were embroidered with alpines. When first married and stricken by joy, she had spent most of her time like a badger, down on all fours, burrowing in the dark earth. She wanted to make a bower for him where he would write his poems. He was delighted with her work. He liked to sit among the scented borders and drink a glass of wine.

Slowly she saw that his work was at an end. She had her own vanity. She meant to make her life a useful thing. She did not have his appetite for squandering. In the end, being practical and in love, she attempted to make her life's work humility.

Oh, love! The loosening force of it. She knew she could have made him work. She had only to pull the pleasantness from under him and he would have taken to verse as a revenge. Instead she hung on, wasting her life, relying on old age to vindicate them. The little retrospective stretch of life must surely acquit its trivia. She imagined them at peace in the garden together, dried out and shimmering like those pearly discs of old growth which are called honesty.

When the doctors told her he was going to get better, she felt no relief. She had done her grieving. Now, some day, she would have to go through it all over again. She had jettisoned trust in favour of the unfriendly skills of survival. Perhaps she was callous. She quite liked the

word, with its suggestion of hard skin. She needed her
hard skin.

After Martha went back to work Jocelyn felt a peculiar
peevishness, which he did not wish to explore. He
telephoned a girl he knew, who was lovely and young
and round.

'Jocelyn!' she cried joyfully. 'What a relief!'

He kissed the receiver, lapping up her maiden youth.

'I thought you were dead,' she said merrily.

There was a goodish pause on the other end of the
line. 'No, no!' he rallied. 'They sent me back. I'm on the
mend, but I'm a prisoner. Come and rescue me. Bring a
bottle.'

'Darling, I can't,' the girl said. 'Actually, I'm dashing
now. Look, it's wonderful that you're better. Do give
me a ring sometime.'

Don't be ridiculous, I am ringing you, he thought in
an apoplexy of irritation. 'I'll do that,' he said warmly.

He telephoned another of his girls.

He imagined, as he waited, the messenger's silent
glide through polished halls, the summoning bells, the
harem's pheremone calm. What had they thought when
she first came to them with her skin the colour of cider
and her unsuitable blue eyes? They must all have been in
love with her.

'Oui?' uttered a cracked voice of entrancing indifference.

'Gertie? It's Jocelyn!'

'Bonjour, Jocelyn,' she said with enduring politeness.

'Aren't you surprised to hear from me? I should be
dead by now.'

'Perhaps you weren't ready for death,' Soeur Gertrude
said.

'What is one supposed to do then, to get ready?'

'Are you really all that keen,' she wondered, 'for death?'

'No, Gert, it isn't that.' He sighed. 'I seem somehow to have offended people. Everyone's gone off me. I've no visitors. Do you know, Martha's gone and left me – gone back to work. It's as if I'd done something unforgivable. I should have gone ahead and died. People were just waiting for the obituary.'

Soeur Gertrude, in her solitary darkness, gave one of her famously economical smiles to think he still saw himself in headlines. 'Maybe Jocelyn Fowler has died,' she suggested.

'Who's left then?' he said fearfully.

'Who knows.'

'I'm bloody lonely, Gert,' he said.

'It is not uncommon,' she assured him. 'Our Saviour on the cross has also mentioned this experience to me.'

'I'm glad someone understands,' he said sourly.

'Yes. Oddly enough, I do. There is a common belief that Our Lord sent His only son on earth to redeem the world, as a supreme sacrifice. In fact, of course, it was envy. By depriving His creatures of paradise, He had given them access to an experience which He had no means to share. He could hardly be God if He was excluded from the privilege of suffering.'

'Damn it to hell,' Jocelyn thought wearily as he put down the phone. 'She's gone nuts.'

He could not shake off his uneasiness in regard to something she had said. In the end he had to crawl out of the bed and drag himself to a mirror to reassure himself with his reflection. The handsome lines of brow and jaw seemed scratched upon the glass. The outline was that of a tree in which strange creatures made their nest and the largest of these was self-pity. 'I'm lonely,' he appealed.

The figure in the mirror mimed mournfully.

'The moping owl does to the moon complain,' he balefully reflected.

About a week after this Soeur Gertrude, unknown to anyone save her silent companions in the cloister, passed away, and Jocelyn Fowler, at the age of fifty-seven and not at all a well man, propped himself up in bed and started, once more, to write.

# Technical Difficulties
# and the Plague

The things women do to their children. I know a woman who called her children Elgar and Mozart. Elge and Moze, they are now. But children can be cruel too.

I called my children Robin and Rosemary, nice names for nice children. It suits their pink cheeks and the light curl of their gold-brown hair. I can say without exaggeration that I gave up everything for them. I gave up the chance of a good career and stayed with my husband, who was never the life and soul of the party. After all that, what do you think they did? They never came.

I don't often brood but I am sitting alone at a cafe in a foreign country and a strange man has just sat down beside me, so you can excuse my mind for running riot. Robin and Rosemary. Their little ghosts do not haunt me but I feel the weight of their ingratitude. I waited so long for them. Everything was ready. I had my insides checked out. They were like a new pin. My husband had his sperm inspected for short measure, but he had been packed to capacity. The little bastards simply couldn't be bothered to turn up.

There is something familiar about the man but I expect that's just my imagination.

You know how it is when you're on your own in a strange place; first there is the giddy freedom. Then you start peering into your handbag. After that you begin imagining things about the people around you.

What annoyed me about Robin and Rosemary is the fact that they were so much Desmond's children – not really mine at all. That business of keeping me waiting, they got that straight from their father. All through our marriage he has been vanishing on mysterious errands, leaving me sitting at home or in the car, or God knows where. He says he has to go and buy a paper or get some money or relieve himself, but he takes so long one feels he must have negotiated the purchase of Times Newspapers or held up the bank. Who knows what he does to relieve himself. Once I accused him of spending time with other women. His response irritated me so much that I seriously thought of leaving him. 'Who'd have me?' he said, and he laughed at both of us.

You won't guess where I am now. I am on the Piazza del Campo in Siena, at that restaurant with the blue and white awning and tables on the shady side of the square. It is a sunny spring morning and we came here to have a look at the Etruscan Museum and then a lunch of asparagus at Guido's. Suddenly Itchy Britches got up and said he had something to see to. 'Don't be long,' I begged him, but you might as well ask Dustin Hoffman not to be short.

This man who has sat down beside me is not unlike Dustin Hoffman. He is dark with a kind of nervous mouth that twitches into a smile when he catches me looking at him. He smokes a lot. In spite of his nervousness he does not look away.

He has a way of holding one's gaze, of drawing you deep into those Amaretto-coloured eyes. People change but their eyes never change. At first I didn't recognize him because of his clothes. He is much richer than he used to be, bits of Gaultier and Cartier stuck all over him. It was only when I found myself wandering into those pools of peat-coloured velvet and I suddenly tripped over my own entrails that I realized who had sat down beside me. 'Jesus Christ,' I muttered. The man laughed. Giorgio – that's his name – laughed. It gave me a chance to compose myself. I leaned back, took one of his cigarettes and held my hand steady to light it. 'Hi!' I said. He beamed at me (that slightly rueful, vaguely wolfish grin) – : 'Don't I know you from somewhere?' Two can play at that game. I studied him, as if my life was an endless queue of Dustin Hoffman lookalikes awaiting identification. 'Somewhere,' I said remotely. 'Well, you're looking good,' he laughed.

Now that is the truth. In spite of everything I look all right. I'll tell you something. Any woman can look terrific. All you need is a lot of money. I got that from my parents.

I deserved it after what they did – or rather, tried to do – regarding my upbringing. Well, they died young, which shows that there is a God in heaven. Anyway, you have to get your hair done once a month at the most expensive place in town, and tip too much which ensures you are always dealt with by the head honcho. You need four trips to the sun a year. My legs are brown all year long. They never peel. You have to have fantastic clothes. Men say they don't notice clothes and it's true. It's not the clothes they notice but a total effect. Getting the right clothes is my neatest trick. I go into one of those expensive boutiques where the girls are always dressed in tight pants and angora sweaters with silver inserts, and I say: 'Look, I'm having an affair with this amazing guy and I need something really special to wear.' Young girls are very creative in the arena of sex. They take on the part and pick out something for you as if they were the ones having the affair. They're used to the clothes. They know how they sit. Depend upon it, you'll walk out with something good. There is a drawback to this sort of transaction. Quite often the girls are very forward and will ask you questions of an intimate nature. I find it's best to just invent a whole scenario, because otherwise they lose heart and will dump you with something in apricot pleated chiffon which makes your bottom look like a pyjama case.

Today I am wearing black linen with big bone buttons, open almost to the thigh. There is a clunk of gold jewellery on one shoulder and my hair partially hides this from view.

My hair comes down in very pretty strings of mouse and yellow colour with intriguing threads of silver and gold. On top it looks as if it was caught in the wind, but only in the right direction. My face is doing well for its age. I have a slight squint, but men seem to find this attractive, and small neat white teeth and a plump sort of mouth.

I wish my husband could see me now. The way this handsome foreigner — my ex-lover in case you hadn't guessed — is looking at me, would drive even the most yellow-blooded husband to a frenzy of fury. He has ordered coffee and brandy for us and is talking about Siena, but his eyes are saying that somewhere under that thatch of rumpled-looking brown hair there is a hand reaching out to undo the next button on my skirt and slide in to feel the skin of palest primrose silk which is all there is between me and decency.

Do lovers know when seduction begins? He is telling me about the Palio, but every word he uses is passion, frenzy, sweat, climax. His brown hand beats the table as he talks of rolling drums and clanging bells, of plot and prayer and pantagruelian feasts.

Swirling through the ancient streets come mace bearers, flag bearers, trumpeters, palace musicians; captain, centurians, district representatives, drummers, flag bearers, pages. There are the knights of the Lion, Bear, Strong Sword, Viper and, of course, the Cock. By the time the riders enter, the surging crowd is delirious with excitement. 'But it only lasts a minute,' I say, 'the Palio. What do all those people do afterwards?'

'They get drunk,' he says. 'They go home and make love.'

'All those poor tourists,' I shake my head; 'having to go home to Stockholm and Texas and Hong Kong and Canberra to make love.'

He laughs. 'They should come to live in Siena like me.'

'Oh, you live here now?' I am all coyness and politeness. Who writes the lousy scripts?

He is lucky enough, he tells me, to live right inside the walls on the Via della Galluzza, a preserved medieval street spanned by eight arches draped with authentic washing. His little house is dark, so he has chosen three small pieces of art — a terra cotta urn from the Roman period, a fifteenth-century manuscript and a small religious painting attributed to Sodoma — and illuminated only these.

'The effect,' he says, 'is . . . intimate. I think you would like it.'

'Are you saying you'd like to show me your etchings?'

'No,' (How can so bad a man manage to look so ingenuous?); 'I'd like to make love to you.'

Strolling beside him across the square which is not a square but the shell of a scallop, I remember what it was about him that delighted and enraged me. Giorgio was never in a hurry. Having made me ready for love he seems to have forgotten he ever mentioned it. He has separated himself from me. He is showing off. He asks me how well I know Siena. Siena is a convent, he says,

Florence a salon, Venice a whorehouse. Do I know Lorenzetti's 'Madonna of Milk' in the Archbishop's Palace? Have I ever used that slot machine in the cathedral that gives you an English commentary when you put in a coin? He has treats in store for me. Treats. His teeth flash on the word. I could kill him.

Time is not as important now as it used to be. I seem to have put in half a lifetime of waiting. When I was young it was everything. Opportunities came like comets, burning themselves out in a blazing trail. Even memory turns to ash. I can scarcely remember my time with Giorgio, except as a little ache of regret and some even tinier twinge of irritation.

What went wrong? We could have been married. Think what our children would look like.

All the same, I can see why he would earn his place in the Good Lovers' Guide. He is clever. He is a tease. When I ask a question he pretends he cannot hear and leans so close my mouth is on the hair that curls softly around his ear. When he guides me across the street, his hand is on the base of my spine, almost on my backside. He may have forgotten that he invited me to be seduced, but he makes it impossible for me to forget.

By now you must be wondering what happens when my husband gets back. Believe me, I would be grateful for a small fit of jealous rage. He'll have a drink, look at his watch, order something to eat. If I haven't returned by the time he's eaten, he'll have another drink, start falling asleep and then go back to the hotel for a siesta. When I get back he'll ask me if I had a nice day.

To hell with husbands. We step out of the sunshine and into the chill of the Duomo. It takes a moment of getting used to, like when you first slide into bed and the cool sheets electrify your skin. The sweat beneath my arms goes cold, my slippery feet begin to reassert their grip on sandals.

Then comes a rush of heat as Giorgio turns to kiss me. Right there in the blazing gloom of the cathedral, with crepe-soled tourists and evil-eyed old black-clad women, his lips are on mine and it is like the first taste of a fresh fig. I am crippled by want. I cannot move. He strides off between the black and white striped marble pillars, which make a perfect designer backdrop for his soft wool clothes. I run to catch him. The feeble clap of my sandals proclaims the weakness of my sex. He is making a phone call, no, putting money in something. I touch his arm. Instead of the embrace I need, he is clamping earphones on my head.

The device is ordinary enough. A selection of slides appears on a screen and a commentary gives you all the most boring details — which century, what pope, how valuable. But the voice! This is the English commentary and the voice is that of the young queen at her coronation — a butterfly packed in ice. I am mesmerized, I am outraged. Is this his idea of a joke, to invade me with virgin purity so that I will feel like the sordid sweaty tourist I am? I glare at him. He is smiling, the bastard. The young queen is telling me about the construction of the New Duomo. It was a fantastic project, intended to cover the whole area of the Campo. Heaven was to be pierced by the spire, tall and blinding with its stripes of black marble and layers of squinting windows.

Great slabs of black marble flew on their high scaffolding like fragile compact discs. Wafers of glass quivered and snapped in the breath of a capricious God.

Why do people always want the impossible? You might as well ask why love never lasts. But that is not the problem. When a love affair ends, there is no more to be said. The real question is, why do love affairs fail to end? Look back on any you've been lucky enough to suffer, and you'll never be able to remember what went wrong. You can waste a whole lifetime in retrospective rehearsals, trying to locate some tiny draught that snuffed out the inferno, convinced that but for that dress or this word, you could have had happiness as long as you lived.

I look at Giorgio with his amused grin and his brown self full of essential maleness as a truffle is full of its fragrance. My perfect twin. He even knows how to take the starch out of me, how to make me female and vulnerable. I am wistful and quivering, in need of making love as much as sex. How did it end?

'Unfortunately it never reached completion,' the young queen is telling me, although of course she is talking about the Duomo. 'This was due to technical difficulties . . . and the plague.'

I have an unfortunate laugh. I holler. Giorgio still has his wry smile but I holler.

One hundred and seventy-two popes and thirty-six emperors gaze down at me furiously from the walls.

Afterwards we plod up the steep streets through the Jewish quarter, past the church of San Girolamo, and the Via dei Servi to the church of St Mary of the Servants and the Piazza Allesandro Manzoni. From here, the whole city is laid out like a delicate antipasto, the little pink roof tiles as dainty as overlapped slices of carpaccio. The spire of the Duomo is a pencil sketch by Ruskin beneath a stockinged lens of a sky.

As you get older you need a lover to aid long-distance vision, the same way you need glasses. Your sight gets clouded by specks of disaster. You see a child walking on a wall, trying to kill itself. You notice some woman, who has been wrenched and wrung by sorrow until even her feet won't set themselves down straight, and you think 'My God, she's younger than me.' The protection of an admirer makes all these things irrelevant and therefore invisible. I suppose there is violence and discontent and poverty and jealousy in the narrow streets that lead down to the Campo, but all I can see is a vision of heaven. There is a faint nagging irritation behind the bridge of my nose, but you get that from wearing spectacles too.

The celestial effects department have also been at work in Giorgio's little house. The lighting is lovely. Imagine a cathedral that was warm instead of cool, that had soft furniture to sink into, that led on to a flowery courtyard behind. It's like a painting – a Turner – where nothing quite exists but is defined by light. I suppose it might seem gloomy in different circumstances.

He tells me to take off my dress and leaves me on a black sofa while he goes to open some wine. Brown skin and primrose silk panties look lovely in this light.

He brings wine that glows like candlelight. We kiss until I reach a slow rolling boil and then he takes off his clothes and what remain of mine. Unencumbered by worldly goods and hand in hand and toe to toe, we are about to fly into heaven.

'You know,' Giorgio smiles, 'this doesn't feel quite right.'

'It feels right to me,' I say as nicely as possible. 'What's the matter?'

He removes the top half of his torso from mine and bends to the floor for his glass of wine. 'I don't know your name.'

The nagging in my nose spreads upwards and becomes a pulsing band across my forehead. 'Call me Mrs Henebry, Giorgio,' I say. 'That's my married name, if that's what you wanted to know.'

'All right, Mrs Henebry,' he says slowly: 'but my name's not Giorgio. It's Leonardo.'

Giorgio has commenced a feathery, circular massage

but the magic has gone. I can't concentrate. I can't stand a mean-spirited man.

'Listen!' I sit up so rapidly that his chin hits my forehead. 'You don't have to protect yourself from me. You don't have to change your identity in case I have you traced or something. I'm not after you − not this time.'

'It's all right, dear Mrs Henebry,' Giorgio strokes my hair. He kisses my eyes. 'I only want to make you happy.'

He's a complex sort of person. I suppose I should enjoy myself, since I don't often get the chance. I'm not young and vulnerable any more. Why the hell should I care about his games so long as I have the company of his pleasure? All the same, I feel I owe it to my younger and more fragile self not to let him get away with it. He hasn't even bothered to change his lines. 'I only want to make you happy.' That's exactly what he said to me the first time.

'Why didn't you marry me, Giorgio?' I say. 'When we were young?'

He gives me an odd, assessing sort of look. 'It is a pity, but alas I did not know you then.'

'How much does it take to know me? You took away my innocence. I gave you my trust.'

He sits up. He shrugs. Naked, he lopes off to look for cigarettes. 'I don't know what you are playing at, but I have never met you in my life before.' When he returns he perches on an edge of the furniture and lights a cigarette. He is back in his leisurely mood. He seems to have forgotten there is a naked woman waiting for him on the sofa. 'You know, Mrs Henebry,' he says; 'you worry me a little. Perhaps you are the kind of woman who makes love to a man and afterwards says she was raped. I think maybe you take your fantasies a little too seriously.'

'What do you mean fantasies, Giorgio?' By now I am furious. 'You think it's some sort of fantasy that we met in Florence as students and you made me your lover and promised to marry me?'

'My name is Leonardo.' He leaves his cigarette poised in his mouth while he bends to retrieve his trousers from the floor and puts them on with a carefulness that indicates an appreciation of his own body. The fall of brown hair over his forehead still tugs at my heart. 'I am thinking,' he says, 'perhaps you are a little confused.'

'Confused?' I reach out and smack him smartly across the face. It isn't the word. It's the awful sliding sense of déjà vu.

All day he has been undermining me but now he has taken me right back. Suddenly I remember everything. Naturally I was confused. I was nineteen and an orphan and had given him all my confidence. I kept nothing from him. 'It was Aunt Lilian, wasn't it? That's why you left me. It was after I told you about our family skeleton – poor loony Aunt Lil. You thought our children might turn out to be nut cases. You thought I might have caught the weird streak.'

He gets up quickly and walks across the room, shrugging into his shirt, buttoning up, protecting himself. 'You're crazy,' he mutters.

There comes a point in life (I believe this happens to most women) where you simply are not prepared to put up with one more single piece of insulting behaviour from any man whatsoever. Feeling perfectly calm, I climb off the sofa and silently cross the floor, pluck the terra cotta urn from the Roman period out of its illuminated niche and break it over the back of his head. It is heavy. I didn't think it would break. 'Sorry,' I say to the figure on the floor, 'about the urn.'

★

Later on, back at the cafe on the Campo, I wonder if he was alive or dead. There was an oddly permanent look to his expression of surprise. Thinking about that *maschera*, I begin to wonder if it really was Giorgio. The eyes were definitely the same, but now I seem to recall that Giorgio had a deep cleft in his chin.

However, there are other things to preoccupy me. I see Desmond lumbering across the square in the afternoon heat. I am almost glad to see him. I will overlook his awful jacket like an ice-cream salesman's, his squeaky shoes and the thinning patch on top of his head. To look at me nobody would believe that I was waiting for such a second-rate specimen of the male sex but we have been through a lot together. We are veterans of the fertility clinic.

'Where the hell have you been?' I say quite amiably when he slumps opposite me at the table.

Do you know what he does? He doesn't even answer me. He gets up and moves to the next table.

I stand over him like a spider and thump the table until the little wrapped sugars jump in their bowl. 'Desmond?' I say; 'speak to me.'

He looks embarrassed and unhappy, the miserable coward. 'Look,' he whispers, 'you're making a mistake. My name isn't Desmond.'

'Go on,' I yell, commanding an audience as I intend to. 'Tell me now you're not my husband.'

I'm reminded of a figure in a painting by Munch as he flees across the square, his cream jacket flapping, his hands raised in dismay. I feel no remorse. Why would he not have the guts to just say straight out he is not my husband when that is the truth? Actually, for a minute I thought it was Desmond. The light has gone round and the sun is in my eyes.

When I was very young I used to think you could

make things happen. I know better now. I was sixteen and entombed in wealthy suburbia by two parents so dull that it is distasteful to think of their part in my existence. I wanted to try my wings, to experiment with life. My parents thought I was crazy. They observed me like a specimen under glass. They wanted me to *see* someone, they said.

What they really wanted was to have me put away. Sadly, they perished in a fire which also took all traces of the ugly house.

After that I thought it was just a matter of getting on with life but I never met anyone to match my pace. I was just passed from one set of fatally indecisive hands to the next, like a bucket in a fire line, destined never to reach the blaze. I waited for my life, for my lover, for my children.

Most of all I waited for my husband whose absences are of such duration and assortment that sometimes, sitting in this hotel lobby or that square, watching the cast change or the weather run through its repertoire, I find myself wondering if he really exists at all.

# The Little Madonna

Look at this. I found it in *The Sun*. It's about a sixteen-year-old called Dolores and her three-month-old daughter, Marigold. 'The Little Madonna', they called her. She has a perfect heart-shaped face and rosebud lips that curve up into a sweet smile. The baby's face was a miniature heart with the same rosebud. Dolores had no job and no one to support her. She was given a council flat. People brought her money and food. Everybody looked forward to seeing her out with the baby, her hair neatly tied in a bunch on top of her head, the baby's scraps of fluff tied up in imitation. Dolores wore a long Indian caftan and the baby had a little Indian smock over her pram suit. People agreed it made you think the world wasn't so bad when you saw them out together. A Mr Cecil Dodd, who owned the shop across the road, said it changed your mind about the female sex.

One day the Little Madonna put the baby out in the playground in her pram because she wanted to take a rest. It was Mr Dodd, rubbing a clear patch on his shop window, wondering if the papers would be delivered on such a day, who saw a ghostly hump beyond the railings of the flats. The pram was completely covered in snow and although his heart hit off his rib cage when he sprinted out to see, he told himself it was only foolishness, no one would put a child out on such a day.

'There!' he reassured himself when he reached the

pram for there was only a toy – a little white woolly bear. It looked so cold he had to touch it and his finger traced beneath the rasping surface, a small, cold slab of forehead, a heart-shaped face, milky blue. His first thought was to wonder who had done it and what they had done to Dolores. He banged on her door, but it was open. She was lying on the floor, near a radiator. He knelt beside her and stroked her face. She opened her lovely gentle eyes: 'I was having a sleep. It was cold so I lay down by the radiator.'

'The baby . . .!' he said.

'It's all right,' Dolores smiled. 'She didn't suffer. I read that people who freeze to death just get very sleepy and then drift off with no pain. I was very careful about that.'

Mr Dodd told this story in court, in support of Dolores's character, even though the inquest had revealed a dappling of long, plum-coloured bruises underneath the little Indian shirt.

The report in *The Sun* is more economical. You have to read between the lines. 'Baby Freezes while Mum Snoozes,' it says. Had the baby failed to freeze to death, she would have been a Miracle Baby, but that is beside the point.

I have this propped up against the milk jug while I'm eating my breakfast. I'm trying to work it out. Who would leave a sixteen-year-old to look after a baby? I remember Rory, who was a good child and sensible, relatively, cut her wrists very neatly with a razor blade when she was sixteen. Being an intelligent girl she read up some books first to make sure the slits would not go through, but it was a very bad moment for me and she meant it to be.

I am not young. I'm a has-been. I'm on the heap and let me tell you this, it's quite a comfortable place to be.

When my womb packed up I went through a sort of widowhood although my husband was not yet dead. I went around sighing, drinking cups of tea to wash down the nerve-stunning pills I bought from a doctor. For a mother to learn that she can have no more children is for a surgeon to have his hands cut off. What can she do? You can't make the children you have last indefinitely. After a long time it came to me that the void was not in my stomach at all. It was in my head. The womb does not have a brain, but that is like saying that the rat is not an intelligent creature. It comes programmed with the cunning of survival. When a young girl presents herself and her head full of dreams to her lover it is natural for the womb to say, 'Let me do the thinking, dear. You just use your pretty head for painting your pretty face.' That's how it is. No, excuse me. That's how it was.

This emptiness I located in my head was not new. It had been there since I was a young woman, Rory's age. My hands were full and my lap. I used my intelligence as a rat does, to plot a path through the maze. Now that the high walls of the maze had crumbled I found myself in open fields. Thoughts rose up into my head. I realized that the period of mourning which succeeds the menopause is not a grieving. It is the weariness that follows upon the removal of a tyranny. Now I was free. I made up my mind never to cook again and became an enthusiastic collector of complete meals in plastic bags with added vitamins. I began, recklessly, to allow entry to thoughts that were not my immediate concern – none of my business at all, to be perfectly frank.

I gave up *The Guardian* which was still telling me how to raise my children and my political consciousness. I started buying *The Sun* which told me about homicides and sex scandals and the secret vices of the royals and reminded me how bountiful women's breasts were. It was the start of my expanded thinking. Every day I find a new marvel on which to ponder.

Why, I ask myself this morning, would anyone leave a sixteen-year-old in charge of a baby? What about all those people who said they brought gifts of food? Why didn't they sneak inside and offer to change the baby's nappy to see if it was being fed all right or if it was being beaten? Who would leave a baby with a sixteen-year-old?

And it comes to me, quite suddenly, sprouting out of the scrap-heap of my middle-aged head – God did. God the Father! He gave His only son to a girl of fifteen. There, with my cup of tea in one hand and my fag in the other, I am filled with alarm as if there is something I should instantly do. I can see the baby with his nappy on backwards as his mother puts henna in her hair. He's crawling around on his hands and knees in his father's carpentry shop, his little mouth full of nails, waiting with growing hopelessness for his mother to come and make him spit them out. Oh, God.

Now there's a thing just caught my eye. 'Orgy and Bess' is the heading. It's about an heiress, Bess Hichleigh-Harrow, who is alleged to have offered the sum of £10,000 to any man who could make her experience an orgasm. She looks a nice ordinary woman. Her coat is good.

There is a great preoccupation with orgasms in the modern world, their frequency, their intensity, their duration. Why choose a muscular spasm as an obsession and not something full of mystery, like a bat or a bee? Why not blame the orange for failing to make us happy and fulfilled?

Because it comes to us from our lover, our husband, our mate, our enemy, with whom all things become possible – whose fault everything is.

Of all the things that rose up in my mind after my womb folded up, orgasms wasn't one. I thought of Rory's bottom, when she was a baby – that hot, clothy acquiescence, serene as a Rajah on its throne, pissing indifferently over her legs and my arms while her own arms, entirely dignified and intelligent, patted my face.

She came in the morning. I called her Aurora – a rosy dawn. I was flabbergasted. At long last, after all the false promises, the beloved had come and she came from myself who, being young, I also loved. Men marvel at rockets to the moon and are not astounded by the journey of a sperm to the womb, the transformation of liquid into life. Only women are amazed. 'I'm not pregnant, not me, I can't be!' they tell the doctor. 'Why me?' they rail at God, and are further dismayed when the emergent infant shows no gratitude to its host, but shits and spits and screams like the devil.

Rory was not like that. She loved me, not just in the way little girls love their mothers, but with the deep earnest love that some men have for their wives, which also contains a small element of contempt. Unlike other children she respected me as the bearer of her life but she thought of me as a simple, shallow person, out of touch with reality. I tried to get myself in shape. I read Freud and Kate Millet and Carl Jung and *The Guardian*. It wasn't easy keeping up. Rory grew up in the 'seventies when everything happened.

I was full of curiosity about the new woman; to be free of priests, to see the penis as a toy, to open one's body to men and lock the door of the womb. 'Tell me,' I coaxed her. Do you know what she told me?

'You were lovely,' she said, 'before Daddy died. Why did you have to change?' My generation were the essential women. We were structured to our role and submitted without grievance. That's what she said. We gave birth in our season without ever giving it a thought. That's what she thinks.

She remembered me in a flowered apron and high-heeled shoes, dabbing on my powder – slap, slap, slap – so that it sat on my nose in a comfortable, dusty way, like icing on a bun. A bright, dry, crimson lip was put on, like a felt cut-out and then blotted on to the lower lip and then the glorious gold compact with its wavy edges was snapped shut with a sophisticated clack, and slipped into a little black bag.

'Remember?' she said. There were tears in her eyes.

Rory comes to visit me once a week although she is not comfortable in the heartless flat I bought after her father died. I hide *The Sun* under a cushion, but she finds it. 'What can you be thinking of?' she asks in exasperation.

She is thirty-two. There are lines around the edges of her eyes and her jaw is starting to set, which is an unnerving thing to see on your own child. So I tell her: 'I was thinking of the Virgin Mary!' I light a cigarette but I have to hold it away at an angle because she doesn't like the smoke.

I suppose the point of it all was that she was only fifteen. Who else could an angel of the Lord have declared unto? I wonder now, why people make such a fuss about the virgin birth? As if making love had anything to do with having babies. What do you suppose she said to her mother and father afterwards? 'I'm going to be the mother of God!'? 'I'm pregnant!'?

'I saw an angel'. I'll bet that's what she said. Afterwards, when she remembered, she told them what the angel said, that like any old mother everywhere, she had conceived of the Lord.

What on earth did her mother say, her good Jewish mother from the house of David who had gone to such trouble to make a nice match for the child? Don't tell me she took it on the chin. An easy lay and a liar, yet! She was too old to have her daughter's faith, but if she had, she would have asked: 'What was its wing span?'

'Look at this!' Now that Rory has pulled my *Sun* out from under its cushion the gloves are off. ' "Bag Baby Found in Bin"!'

This is my favourite story today. It's about Norman who was found in a bag which was then stuffed down into a bin. It is a large denim shoulder bag, well enough worn to be prudently discarded. Baby Norman seemed to accept this as his world, or hiding place, and was angry only when disturbed. He has a very red face with rough patches like a butcher's hands. He is not winsome. The item is an appeal for his mother to come back and claim him but his mother has ditched dour Norman, she has sacrificed her battered denim shoulder bag which she probably quite liked, and callously pinned the name 'Norman' on his little vest. She has put the tin lid on him and she is never coming back.

Now I've made my daughter miserable. She says I am growing morbid. As you grow older you see things differently. Cause, you realize, is only the kite tail of effect and God is a lateral thinker. I heard a Chinese fable once which said that fate bestows a gift for life on every child at birth. Perhaps Baby Norman's gift was to be left in a bag. Someday, when he is an ugly man being reviled by a woman, he will tell her that his mother left him in a bag in a bin, and her heart will break and she will take him on. He would have been ugly with or without his mother's indifference, but who else would have loved him if his mother had? Rory says you can't believe anything you read in *The Sun*. I suppose she's right, yet she believes absolutely and without a wisp of doubt that Mr Gorbachev is ready to lay down all his arms.

There is only one mystery left in life, or at any rate in the Western world, where people have opened out the brain and the soul, analysed the body's responses and claimed for themselves in everything from work to love to life or death, the right to choose. Only the child remains the unchosen one. Who knows whether twin soul or tyrant comes dimpling from the neck of the cervix? Cells gather inside us in secret like a pack of dogs or a flock of angels. It could be the Messiah. It could be the man in the moon. Only a child would open Pandora's Box.

Only a Marigold or little Norman's mother would have the nerve to shut it again.

Rory is right. I was lovely before. I made lemon drops and shepherd's pies and fairy cakes. Women play house to preserve a moment that once was almost theirs, the same way they paint their faces to hold youth a little longer. My husband used to tell me – or tried to tell me – over and over, about a trip in a canoe with his father when he was seven. That's all I remember except for official reports issued daily over the tea table. For all I knew about him he might have been a fish in a bowl. I told this to Rory but she thought I was criticizing him. 'You made your choices,' she said. And I have.

I used to think that Rory would be my guide dog when I went over the hill, would lead me into the new generation.

Now I see that she was hanging around waiting for me to give her the vital information she needed to grow up. We have nothing to do with each other except love and guilt. The terms of reference change with the times and experience is wear-dated. She thinks I turned to packet foods and tabloid papers because I lost interest in life. In fact it is my interest in life that impels me to labour-saving food and literature – that and an aversion to eating anything that still looks like an animal, although I am too old now for the full routine of nuts and pulses. I talked to an Indian on the bus one day (you have to pick your company with care if you intend to say anything you mean) and told him how I could no longer bear to pick up a fish or a chicken and take it home and eat it, because I suddenly knew they were my brothers, but now I worried that such thinking might in due course lead to a meatless world in which the pleasant cow would become extinct. 'But the vast, intensified brotherhood of cows is ruining the ozone layer with its communal breaking of methane wind,' the Indian gentleman enlightened me. I found this exchange deeply satisfactory. How fitting for the Almighty to knock us all off with a massive cow fart.

What appeals to me now is the language of the tabloid. People do not fornicate or have carnal knowledge. They have sex romps. They frolic. They do not exceed the permitted number of alcohol units. They guzzle. 'He Guzzled Bubbly while he Peddled Death,' ran the banner headline above the story of a drugs dealer.

It is not, after all, a chapter of adult corruption but a nursery story of miracle babies and naughty children looking for pleasure or treasure, excitement or escape, and reigning over all is the breast goddess – the giver of forgiveness, of guzzling and joy.

Have we all been let down by our mothers who failed to frolic while we guzzled? Was little Marigold lucky, in spite of the bruises and her cold sleep, to have, for a little while, a mother young enough to romp? If only we had the right to choose.

I have a secret. When you get to my age, your fingers go numb and they lose their grip and then you can choose anything you fancy.

There is a photograph in my secret box of a man and a woman. They are not my parents because I was not born then, but I have chosen them. They do not smile. They watch the camera as if it was a test. The girl clasps her flowers like a doll. She has a dress with square buttons and a hat which claps its brim over her alarmed eyes. The man has a suit but he does not wear it, he is worn by it. Such pure people. When this is over, will they be allowed to take off their good clothes and play again?

After the wedding my mother told me they ate rashers and eggs in a hotel and drank champagne and then went to Blackpool on the boat.

In my mind's eye that is where I see them, leaning on the rail looking into the water that floated them away from the world of rules and responsibilities. They might have played 'I spy' or talked about the enormous meal they would eat when they got to their hotel – chicken and salad and soufflé and wine – for they were thin and were probably always hungry. Now and again the boy might have looked at the square buttons on the pale blue dress and thought: she's underneath there and she's my woman now. It is certain that they did not think about me for I did not exist then, just as they do not exist now, and did not exist after I was born and made them grow up. It is almost certain that they did not think about orgasms although they might have kissed and kissed until they were in an ecstacy of deprivation. They might have thought that ecstacy was just a tiny little moment away – a romp, a frolic, away – like the jam at the bottom of the pudding dish when you had eaten most of your rice.

Most likely they just thought that they had all the time in the world now; that they never, ever had to please anyone for the rest of their lives but themselves and one another, which were one and the same; that for tonight they might just hold each other close on the narrow bunk and rock to slumber on the waves and tomorrow, in private, in another country, start off their lives.

# L'Amour

The trouble began because I was an animal lover. I mean to say, that was the source of all our troubles. I was taken from my role of son at the age of eight by the death of my mother. 'Angels lead our sister into paradise,' said the minister but I was left behind on earth with my father and my mother's cat which was blind in one eye and had a fungal infection of the fur, but we hadn't the heart to put it down.

My father and I did not know what to do with each other. We had never taken much notice of one another, being content with the attention of my mother. After her death we abided. At mealtimes we met at table and waited until it became evident that her ghost would not flutter down with meat and pots of mashed potato and then we would rise silently and separately and arm ourselves with jam and cheese and biscuits and things in tins. We did not panic when the food ran out. We recognized my mother as the source of nourishment and comfort and accepted that these had died along with her. After a time my father said to himself: 'The boy is growing. I must see to the business of food.'

He made a jelly. It was constructed in layers of different colours. Each shade had to be allowed to set before another layer was applied. It took several days to complete and was displayed on a plate on the draining board. In some way or other it did not live up to our expectations and we left it there until it slid down into a pool of its own rust-coloured water.

'What would you like?' my father said.

'I'd like . . . a kitten.'

He bought me two. By the time they were finished leaving puddles under the kitchen table, they were leaving their own kittens in the linen press. I got a donkey from a man in the street by giving him my bicycle. A dog followed me home from school. Boys gave me the things their parents would not allow them to keep — a snake, a pet rat, a poisonous spider. I had a thrush too, that the cats had knocked about a bit and I rescued it. It grew so tame it would sit on my hand and we would whistle at each other. Other birds and less friendly animals lived in secret places in the garden and I climbed trees to look at robins' eggs and lay on my stomach over a muddy pool to watch the sluggish sorcery of frog spawn. I was very keen on them all, even snails with their outer space aerials and their pearly trails. Some of them liked me too and in this way, in due course, I learned to do without my mother.

It was different for my father. He could not adapt. Although it was obvious to both of us that no one could ever take the place of Mother, he began, quite soon after her death, to look for someone who would stand in her place. I don't think he cared what she was like. The ladies he brought home to tea were of such varying quality that he might have chosen them from a bus queue. One of them had cheeks like raw liver dipped in flour and I had to kiss her. 'This is Miss Dawlish,' he introduced, (or on other occasions, Miss Reddy or Miss Frostbite or Miss Havanagila, I think); and his eyes would say: 'Be nice to her.' I was nice to them all. I showed them my snake and my poisonous spider. In spite of this they never came back.

'I believe it is because of the boy's animals,' my father confided to an aunt when he thought I was not listening.

'Of course it is,' the aunt said sharply. 'What free agent would wish to take on a zoo as well as another woman's child?' He never said anything to me. He would no more interfere in my life than I would in his. The stream of ladies ceased and he grew very silent.

One spring, two years after my mother's death, I noticed that he was happy again. He had come back from a business visit to Paris and when he fetched me from my aunt, he was full of energy and jokes, the way he used to be when Mother was alive and they were going to a dance. Shortly after this he paid some more brief visits to Paris and then he asked me if I would like to have a holiday there. I said that I would. I was very interested in Paris. My parents had once had a postcard from Paris and on the back was written: 'Watching the world go by in gay Paree!' (which is how Paris is pronounced there). I thought at the time that it would be phenomenal to be in a place where one could watch the whole world go by.

When Father told me that he had a friend there – a Mlle Duclos – whom he wished me to meet, I took no more notice than I had of the Dawlishes and Frostbites. I was too interested in Paris. A lot of my concentration went on persuading Mrs Crutch, who did our house-work, to feed my pet animals and insects. I got over these difficulties, Father bought me an astonishing suit of clothes which made me look like a man of twenty, and we were on our way.

I was not able to form an immediate impression of Paris for we were taken first to our hotel which was a chateau some distance from the city, where we were to stay and to meet Mlle Duclos. It was a smashing place, full of towers like wizards' hats. A long drive hid its curves under trees and in between the splashes of leaves, the starker branches of a deer's horns made patterns on the sky. I had to press myself against the window of the car to make out that the grey bumps, crouched behind swarms of bluebells, were not stones but baby rabbits. We came to the castle entrance. A conference of important-looking little dogs with ears like wigs ranged about the steps and in the doorway was a princess.

She was the most beautiful lady I have ever seen. A long yellow soft dress with sleeves like butterflies reached almost to her ankles. She was tall but delicate-looking and had a cloud of brown hair. I glanced at my father and could see that he too was under the spell of the castle and its princess. He drove the car with his eyes, very bright, fixed on the lady.

'What do you think, Nicholas?'

'Brillo!' I whispered.

'Precisely,' he laughed.

He stopped the car and got out, seeming to forget about me, which I did not mind. He hurried up the steps and the little dogs stiffened and shouted angrily.

'Darling!' he called.

The princess turned to him and smiled. She held out her arms and he went into them, humbly, like someone receiving a blessing. After they had kissed he turned and summoned me with an excited wave. I scrambled out of the car and ran to her.

'Say hello to Mlle Duclos,' he said.

Nothing had prepared me for this. She bore no more resemblance to the Dawlishes than did the castle to a dog kennel. With an effort I stuck out my hand. 'How do you do, Mlle Duclos?'

She bent to study me and her hair fell down, framing her face. 'You must call me Marie,' she said. 'I think we are going to be friends.' She kept hold of my hand when she straightened and turned to my father. 'He is exactly like you. What a nice surprise!'

I could see immediately why my father looked at her in such a dazed way. In that moment all I wanted was to have her smile on me, her hand in my hand. We went into lunch and sat at a table, all of us smiling. 'No one here knows that my mother is dead,' I thought. 'No one knows we are not a proper family.'

Father and Marie ordered escargots and langoustes. 'What would you like, little picture of your papa?' she whispered to me.

'Chips,' I whispered back.

She pushed my hair from my forehead. 'In France, the children are not treated like little animals, fed with the scraps from the plates of adults. Here, you will learn to dine properly, even with a taste of wine. Have you ever eaten escargots?'

I shook my head. I could see my father looking at me hopefully.

'Have them to please me,' Marie said.

'All right,' I nodded.

'What a nice boy.' She rubbed my hair. 'I don't think I am going to let you go.'

How happy my father looked then, no longer lonely, reaching out to touch her arm while her hand still rested on my head so that we were all joined together like daisies in a chain. Later I wished we could have all died in that moment so that none of us would ever know loneliness again, or fear.

The escargots came; little curls of something on a dish with holes. I ate one and decided that if I thought about something else I could probably finish them. I had got about half way around the holes when Marie leaned towards me and said, in that confidential way that made one dizzy: 'What do you think?'

I smiled and shrugged, my mouth full of buttery rubber.

'Escargots! Do you know what they are?'

I saw that my father looked alarmed when she said this and his anxiety flew to me. 'What are they?' I demanded.

'Ha! Ha!' Her giggle was now like a girl's. An older girl's. 'They are snails, my pet.'

I spat it out. The snail. I felt she had played a terrible trick, not only on me but on my father.

'Nicholas!' my father was horrified but I would not look at either of them. Father kept on chewing until he had eaten all the snails on his dish.

I might have forgotten the incident. Marie looked as upset and bewildered as I did. Then the waiter came carrying three poor creatures that were trying to escape.

'Voilà! Our lobsters!' said Marie in excitement.

'They're alive!' I was horrified.

'Not for long!' Her delicate, teasing laugh rang out as their slow pincers struggled with the air.

I ran out of the restaurant and stayed there, kicking a bed of flowers to pieces until Father came to look for me. 'Dirty foreigners! Filthy foreign savages!' I aimed at the heads of quivering daffodils.

'Marie said I should come.' Father looked miserable. 'She thought she ought to leave us alone. She will join us again later.'

I said nothing.

'Don't you like her?'

I shook my head.

'I thought you seemed happy. I was so pleased,' he said.

'She's a sneak,' I shouted. 'She made me eat a snail.'

'No, no! It is the custom of the country. The animals do not suffer. You must learn to adapt.'

He looked as lost as I did. Neither of us was adaptable. I wondered if, like me, he was remembering my mother's meals, shepherd's pies and rice puddings, food that had long lost its connection with any living source. I thought of her apron and her body beneath it, a fathomless cushion, where one could lie when one was confused, and love came out but she never looked for anything as demanding, in return, as friendship.

In the afternoon Father showed me Paris. He told me about the buildings, places of art and war and opera, dulling the sunny streets with clouds of history. I preferred the cafes and markets, the little batto boats on the river. 'What do you think, Nicholas?' Father said. It was a city of the dead; statues of dead generals by dead sculptors. It reminded me of the place where I had stood in the most inestimable fear with, overhead, the foreign storm of adult weeping and down below, in the ground and powerless to take control, my mother. I said none of this to my father. Instead, I said: 'I'd like to go to the place where you can watch the world go by.'

He brought me to a wide, pretty street with trees and heavy traffic and we sat at a tin table outside a cafe. We ate ice-creams. A lot of people passed, some who hurried and some who seemed to regard the boulevard as a drawing room in their own home but although I looked and looked, there was no change of scenery, no yellow hills of Montana nor snow-capped Swiss mountains. 'It's only a street,' I said indignantly. 'You cannot watch the world from here.' Father seemed not to hear. 'Nicholas!' He leaned forward suddenly, his face as serious as if I was another adult. 'You must make an effort with Marie. In due course I know you will come to love her as I do.'

I was confused by this word, 'love'. 'She's not my mother,' I said.

'She will be a sister – a friend.'

'I have my animals.'

For a moment he was silent. 'I haven't told her,' he said.

We were both desperate. 'Don't let her hurt them,' I said.

'She will accept them but first you must accept her.'

The anxiety in his voice made me nervous. 'What if she does not accept them? What if she had a boy and he had a lot of animals, Father? Would you accept them?'

'I would accept anything that was a part of Marie. I know it is not fair to speak to you like this, Nicholas, but I cannot lose her. I would be lost without her. I know she likes you but if she thought you did not like her she would not wish to intrude. She is a woman of sensibility.'

I thought of her laughing at the lobsters.

'Promise me, Nicholas' – my father spoke urgently – 'that you will be friendly and behave.'

I felt sorry for him. I was going to say yes, I would behave, but he did not wait for my answer. He saw Marie approaching then and he stood and waved to her. He looked like a blind man, blinded by her bright smile and I thought that he was lost with her or without her.

In another moment my resolve became unnecessary for her hand was on my head and her kiss on my cheek and a rush of complicit whispers in my ear and I laughed with happiness.

We were all holding hands again when we moved off. We went to see the Cathedral of Notre Dame, huge and black inside with a big window of many colours 'Like a firework in the night,' Marie said, leaning down, close to my ear.

Later, Father and Marie went into a bookshop called Shakespeare and Company and I stayed outside in the sun and read messages from a glass-covered noticeboard.

*Widower, formerly married to woman with loose dentures,*
*with whom conversation was like water dripping from a*
*stalagtite to stalagmite, seeks quiet girl like Amelia in* Vanity
Fair. It made me wonder if the whole world was full of
widowers in search of ladies to replace their wives? If he
saw Marie would he think she looked like Amelia in
*Vanity Fair?* In my mind, the defect of the widower's
wife transferred to himself, and I saw him with his rainy
teeth, approaching the bookshop in search of his reply.
I looked around quickly. There was no one who resembled the squishy-toothed widower but all the same I
went and stood guard in the doorway in case he should
come along and see Marie and try to claim her.

That night we ate in a restuarant where each dish was
covered in a silver dome. Marie was like a fairy princess
with her hair done up on top of her head and a dress of
something blue and filmy. She and Father drank champagne, giving me a little in a glass, so that by the time
we went in to dinner I was a bit foolish.

The menu was brought — like a huge birthday card
with a picture of wildlife on its cover and each inscription
inside an exercise in calligraphy.

'Something light,' Marie suggested. 'A little pâté or
some cuisses de grenouilles.'

'Kweess . . .?' I giggled.

'Cuisses de grenouilles — frogs' legs!' said Marie with
her lovely smile.

'I'll have the pâté,' I said quickly, hiding my horror. 'I
have tasted pâté.'

'Not this pâté, little one,' she said. 'This is a speciality
— very good. Pâté de grives — thrush pâté.'

'No!' I cried out. I thought of the family of thrushes
in our garden, sunbathing on heaps of mown grass, their
wings spread like fans. They swooped into our peach
tree and called to one another when the fruit was ripe.

'The boy is . . . fond of animals.' Father looked embarrassed. He shot me a yearning glance.

'Of course he is.' Marie was relieved. 'But these are not pets. These are garden pests – frogs and thrushes.'

'I have a pet thrush,' I told her.

'Aah!' She made a face, considering. 'You must tell me about yourself. Everything!'

'I have a dog and a donkey and six cats.'

Father looked as if he was in pain.

'. . . a pet rat and a snake and a spider.'

Marie was nonplussed. She grinned first and then, seeing that I was serious, she shuddered. 'My God, what a ménagerie!' She spoke rapidly to my father in French while I strained to understand but he, seeing my anxiety, gave a little hopeless smile and said for both of us in English:

'I am afraid, my dear, that they are all indispensable. They are his family.'

She sipped her wine and swirled the content of her glass. 'I am afraid of spiders,' she said to herself. 'A donkey! A rat! Mon Dieu!'

When a very long time had passed she turned to me with that bright smile of hers. 'May I join your family, Nicholas?' Father and I laughed with relief and we raised our glasses. 'What a ménagerie!' she said again.

Marie ordered for us all. 'Do you have pet prawns?' she said. I had had a few sips of wine diluted with water by now and I laughed like a drunk old man.

We ate our prawns and made our plans. Marie was going to come and live with us. When she had got the house in order she would work with my father in his antiques business. Sometimes she spoke to Father alone and ignored me as if I was a child, which made me jealous. Sometimes she pretended that Father was an old man and that she and I were the same age. 'Have you

ever had a pony? Your papa is too decrepit to ride a
horse but you and I, Niccy, will have ponies and will go
riding in the fields.'

The argentine domes of our main courses arrived.
Marie lifted one and closed her eyes to sniff. 'Now I
think I have chosen well,' she said. 'A little crispy duck
for your papa and I and for Niccy, a more delicate
fowl.'

'Kentucky Fried Chicken,' I cried cheekily, executing
a mock drum roll upon the dome of my dish with my
knife and fork and making the adults laugh but I retained
enough sense to know that I must not actually allow the
cutlery to touch the silver. I swept up the cover from
my dish. A tiny bird, no bigger than a robin, it seemed,
lay dead and bleeding on to a piece of toast. The shock
was such that I glanced up quickly to see if the others
had noticed but they had lost interest in me and were
busy with their plans. 'No!' I said, but silently. I covered
it up in its silver coffin. Some chips had come with the
main course, and I ate those.

'Have some cheese,' Marie said, when our dishes had
been taken away; 'or would you prefer dessert?'

'No thank you. I'm a bit tired,' I said. 'May I go to
bed now, please?' I had seen a table of delicious sweet
things near the entrance to the restaurant but they
might be hedgehogs covered in whipped cream or
chocolate-coated mice. I slid down from my chair and
left the room quickly before they could argue. In the
doorway I turned and looked back. Their hands were
joined across the table, their faces lit with happiness. I
had not failed my father. He would not lose her. But as I
stood there, feeling brave, straining to see them through
the teasing filter of candle flames, past the wealthy
diners eagerly dissecting small birds and fishes and waiters
scurrying with mirrored prisons of more slaughtered

wildlife, I suffered another shock. It was the realization that I had not allowed myself that last look to assure myself of Father's salvation but for another glimpse, for myself, of Marie.

In bed that night I had a dream.

I was walking up the path to the chateau. I came across a mass of creatures seeking shelter beneath a large tree from the breeze; furry rabbits, baby deer, lobsters, pheasants and smaller birds, shuddering dreadfully. I went to look for the gamekeeper. 'Look at these creatures,' I rebuked. 'They are so cold! See how they shiver. Why are they not properly housed?' The old keeper pointed to the sunny sky. 'Cold? No, my little man. They are watching the approach of the gourmet. They are terrified.'

In the morning I ran to find Marie. She was on the terrace, having breakfast with my father. She put out her arms and I laid my head on her white angora sweater. 'Marie,' I whispered. 'This is a secret. Don't tell my father. Why do French people eat so many little animals? I don't mind the big ones, but the little ones!'

She dipped her roll into coffee and held it out for me to bite the hot, soggy, buttery mass. 'A secret,' she said; 'yes. God put the little creatures on the earth for our pleasure. They know this. They are happy to die for me.'

I believed her. I would have died for her too.

For some reason Father seemed discontented this morning. He remained silent through most of the breakfast and then he said to me: 'We are going out to lunch. Marie's maman will be joining us.' He said it like a challenge, as if he expected me to object. I did not mind. I knew that it was customary for a lady to introduce a prospective husband to her mother and I was surprised my father did not know this.

'If you marry Father,' I said to Marie, 'your mother will be a part of our family too. She will be our gran.'

Marie stroked my hair. 'You are an exceptionally nice and clever boy,' she said; and Father frowned.

Meeting Marie's mother was as much of a surprise as Marie herself had been. She was dressed in black and she was old, old – the sort of old that seems never to have been young, like a parsnip. I could see that Father did not like to think that this ancient root was a source of Marie. Normally when speaking to old people, he made himself seem older to put them at their ease. Now he seemed very young and offhand, a lout. She did not appear to like him either but gave a very insincere little laugh when Marie presented him with breathless pride.

She was put into the back of the car with me and we drove away. For a while she did not say anything but looked out the window. Then she said to nobody in particular, 'He thinks he is on trial but it is I who am on trial.' She gave me a bitter little smile and after that she did not speak until we got to the restaurant.

It was a very pretty place with plates on the walls and thick lace curtains on the windows and in the centre, a long table, covered with tarts. I was put sitting opposite the old woman. My father sat across from Marie, his eyes smiling and his stubborn look gone.

The menu was scrawled in pen on a piece of card. I read it several times over but could find nothing that was not cruel; the oysters eaten live (I once heard that they flinch when you put on the lemon juice), the foie gras of force-fed geese. the veal of imprisoned calves, lobsters boiled alive. 'I'll have melon,' I said miserably and . . . 'steak'; for at least the cow was large and fed a lot of people.

'No, no, dear little peasant,' Marie said. 'Have some oysters. Have them for me.'

'Melon. Melon and fish and chips.' The old woman spoke out, 'I have no teeth to chew and my stomach prefers plain food. Keep me company.'

'All right,' I said and gave a silent sigh of relief that I would not have to eat anything cooked alive.

My father ordered the food and a bottle of wine and some water. He poured wine for himself and Marie while she half filled her mother's glass and mine with water. She took the wine from Father then and used it to top up our glasses. 'Talk to my maman and I will talk to your papa,' she whispered into my ear.

The old woman was looking around the restaurant, tearing pieces of bread from the slices in a basket and chewing on them rapidly.

'I have to talk to you,' I said after a while.

'Well I hope you have something interesting to say.' She lifted up her glass. 'Santé'. She tasted her drink and then puckered her mouth into an old, savage grin. 'Elle a baptisé le vin,' she said with a look of contempt for Marie.

I told her about my animals but I did not think she was very interested. She kept looking around at other guests and seemed most concerned with old ladies of her own age. 'Watch her!' she would jab a finger at a very dainty old woman, dining on her own. 'See her!' She pointed out an ancient creature presiding over a Sunday lunch of several generations. The woman had whiskers and grey hair cut short like a man's and looked almost identical to her old husband who sat beside her.

When the food was brought Marie's mother ate it as a bird eats, her head on one side, considering the tastes. Every so often a jerk of the head towards me and my glass indicated that I should drink the watered wine.

'I'm not very fond . . .' I tried to say. She made a rapid movement with her hand to dispose of my argument. 'Good for the stomach!' she said.

Father and Marie leaned across the table so that their faces were close and they talked together in low voices. They seemed indifferent to the food. They ate very little although they drank the wine.

In a strange way, I felt quite comfortable with the old woman. She spoke to herself, sometimes. When her fish was put before her she stared at it sadly. 'Pusspuss-pusspuss,' she called out hopefully, looking under the table. She pushed the plate aside. 'Des hot dogs,' she said. 'Et des glaces. Avec des noix.' She was dreaming. 'Et des cerises!' Her eyes filled with tears. She looked up then and gave me her sour little grin. I ate a great many chips and drank the Ribena-coloured wine and after a while I got a feeling of exceptional power and peace.

The old woman drained her glass very quickly although each time she drank from it she made a face which suggested she did not like its content. When her glass was empty, Marie would absent-mindedly attend to the mixing of liquids. Granny kept an eye on Marie and on the bottle. She did not look at her the way my mother used to look at me. It was hard to think of her as Marie's maman. She seemed quite removed from her – quite removed from everything, in fact, except the mixture in her glass. When she spoke again it was with a sharp tug at Marie's sleeve. 'The wine is finished!'

Marie gave Father an apologetic smile but he looked understanding and signalled at once for more wine. To my astonishment, the old woman winked at me.

Wine was poured. Father filled glasses for himself and Marie and then they raised them and touched them gently and their eyes had a soft burning look with a gentle light like candles. They moved the glasses, still touching, away from their faces and very slowly their faces touched; their lips.

'They haven't . . .' I was about to protest that they

hadn't put water and wine into our glasses but the old woman placed a bony finger on her lips and eyed me severely. I hung my head and sighed in confusion. A touch made me look up. That same finger was on my head. The old woman was smiling at me the way that adults look at each other when they know something that you do not. She lifted her finger from my head in such slow motion that my eyes were forced to follow it. A corner of her eye watched our kissing relatives. The finger swivelled clockwards and stopped upon the wine. With astonishing speed she seized the bottle and filled both our glasses. She made a motion to me that I should drink it up quickly. I did as I was told, too amazed by her boldness to notice the bitter taste. When I had drained my glass I gave a laugh, a hoarse laugh that sounded strange to me and she nodded and gave an ordinary old woman's laugh.

She raised her eyebrows now, with a little smile for her foolish daughter and my entranced father. Father held Marie's face with the tips of his fingers. Once more the old woman's hand moved slowly over the table and made a catlike pounce on the bottle. As she was refilling our glasses Marie gave a funny little grunt – the sort of noise you would make if cream from an éclair spilled on your chin – and her arm groped sideways and took the bottle from her mother. She held it up to Father and gestured sideways with her eyes to let him know what had happened. Father looked quite shocked but he looked dazed too and when Marie laughed he smiled on us all. The old woman gave him a poisonous smile. Father and Marie returned to their courtship but they kept the bottle on their own side of the table.

'Merde!' said the granny.

'That's a curseword!' I said.

She looked at me scornfully. 'I don't suppose you know any cursewords?'

'I do.'

'Go ahead!'

'It's not allowed.'

'Cul!' she said provocatively.

'That's a terrible word!' I looked around in case anyone might have heard it. I lowered my voice; 'It means your bum!'

'Bum!' the old woman cackled with delighted wickedness. 'You said a bad word. Bum! Bum!'

'That's not a bad word. I know much worse than that.'

'I don't believe you.'

'Shitehawk!' I shouted out.

Father looked around in alarm and confusion, as one woken from a dream. 'Nicholas!'

'Sorry, Father.'

'It's the wine,' Marie giggled.

'Don't worry,' the granny said. 'I can handle him. Pphhh!' — she made a noise to suggest that she was already worn out with handling; 'but not without my medicine!' She held out her glass.

'I don't know!' Marie shook her head; 'two delinquents!' She dealt the glass its watery mixture and left the bottle in the centre of the table.

'That spider of yours,' the old woman said; 'is it poisonous?'

'Of course.'

'How do you know? Has it ever bitten anyone?'

'No!'

'Is it . . . deadly?'

'I think a doctor could save you,' I hazarded.

'Then we must try it out sometime.' She raised her glass to her lips but instead of drinking she merely gestured with it and muttered with a grin, 'du pipi d'âne!'; and then with a conjurer's flick she emptied the mixture into a plant which was on the edge of our table, in a pot wrapped in red crepe paper.

She filled our glasses deftly with unadulterated wine and raised hers once more but instead of the usual phrase she said in a ladylike and barely audible murmur, 'Salaud!' I drew in my breath with excitement and admiration. She managed to make it sound like a harmless salute but this was a really strong curse. A boy in school had told me. It meant . . . bastard!

I gulped from my glass. 'Arseholes!' I hissed.

'Salope!'

'Horsepiss!'

'Zizi!'

'Balls!'

'Trou de balle!'

I drank more wine. It had the colour of cherries, the taste of fruit and fire. It filled my head with wildness and I dared say anything. 'Fff . . .' I drew out the worst word of all, pressing my teeth down into my lower lip.

'Non!' The old lady looked alarmed.

'That's a really bad word, isn't it?' My eyes were sparkling and my head swam. 'I don't care how bad it is, I'm going to say it.'

'I know your word,' she said. 'It is not so bad. It is a very sad word.'

'Sad?' I said with a coarse laugh. 'Do you understand it?'

'Do *you* understand it?'

I understood and I did not. 'It's awfully rude. It has to do with men and women.'

'Ah, yes,' she said. 'L'amour.'

'Love.'

'Love? Non. I prefer l'amour. Your English love is too noble – too full of expectation and disappointment. Too full of duty to parents and country. L'amour is touching and foolish and human.'

She leaned across the table until she was as close to me as Father was to Marie. 'It is –'; she tapped the table for emphasis; '– the miracle of creation in the magic of enchantment. Only a sad man would so curse his frustration.'

The moment passed. It was as if it had never happened. The old woman called out for strawberry tart. She dug her spoon into the glistening humps of fruit and made sounds of appreciation.

She had forgotten me. Worse, Marie had forgotten me. I turned to her in appeal but she was lost to me, far away on some voyage of the heart, safe in the magic of enchantment.

'What are you thinking?' The old woman had finished her tart.

I pretended not to hear. Her foolishness had cost me Marie's attention.

'You are thinking about l'amour. You are thinking you know it all and you are a disillusioned fellow.'

I shook my head crossly.

'You are jealous of my daughter and your father because they have found happiness in each other; because they need no one else.'

'It's true!' I said. 'They're all right. They don't want us.'

'Poor fellow. Have some tart. Already you are a victim.'

I ate the tart. It was glorious.

'There will come a moment in your life,' the woman who looked like a parsnip was saying; 'when you will look at a person the way *they* look at one another and from that moment you will never be free.'

'Then it's a spell! It's a trap!'

'How quickly you are growing up,' she said. 'It is not the spell that is the trap. It is the vanishing of l'amour that imprisons us. Where did it go? How can we live without it?'

'Well . . . how?'

'There is no answer. Whole lives are spent searching for it, trying to entice it back. Look!' She pointed out a beautifully dressed old lady who was dining on her own. 'Do you know who that lady is? That is the dognapper of Paris. Once she was a respectable woman but she fell in love with a man who was married. Love made her disreputable. When he left her she was so lonely she took to stealing little dogs. She has dozens of them in her apartment. Watch her closely! See *her* now!' She turned to point out the whiskery old peasant at whom she had earlier been staring. 'That is the richest woman in France. Her husband still loves her.'

Almost as she spoke the old man at her side turned and said something to her and then he kissed her whiskery, horrible mouth and smiled into her eyes.

'Then Marie and my father must be very rich,' I said.

The old woman shrugged. 'They are gamblers. Their fortune depends on the turn of a card. Marie is very young. When she looks at him she sees in his eyes a mirror of her own perfection. Wait until they each discover that the other is not perfect! Quelle barbe!'

'But Marie is kind! She is willing to put up with all my animals.'

'She is a clever girl. She has thought to herself: "He is growing up. Soon he will be tired of all these rats and spiders. It is not long to wait." Or else she believes she can charm you away from your leggy friends.'

'But my father!' I said. 'What about him? He would do anything for Marie.'

She gave her sour old chuckle. 'We shall see.'

We were all distracted then by a piercing cry. A woman was standing up, shouting for the management, the police. 'Someone has stolen my little dog!' she wailed in French.

I looked quickly for the old lady in furs but she had vanished. Madame Duclos was smiling at her empty plate.

In the morning Father was alone and in a fury. 'That woman,' he said, rattling the grey printed wastes of a French newspaper. 'I have been deceived.'

I knew he was not really speaking to me so I spooned jam on to my bread and drank my milky coffee.

'She intended to bring her mother to live with us. That foul-mouthed old drunkard! Good God! That would be nice company for you, Nicholas.'

'I don't mind,' I said, but he did not hear.

'If there is one thing I cannot and will not tolerate it is deceit. She waited until the very last minute, until all our arrangements had been made, before springing that pleasant surprise. What an idea!'

'What else could she do?' I said, but he was not listening.

I did not see Marie again. We left quite soon afterwards, on our own.

I thought, later on, that the old woman had been both wrong and right. Father did not appear to be in a trap. In fact, he was freer than before. For a while he was in a rage and then he brooded and after that he resumed life with the energy that had seemed to die with my mother. After several years he married a plump Miss Windhouse and he often whistled with contentment.

The animals were gone by then. I thought it best to face up to the fact that it was not normal to spend so much time with stupid creatures. Their dumb faces began to annoy me.

'How would you like to be cooked?' I shouted one day when my thrush was making a racket for food.

All of that is in the past now and I am free to think of other things. In a little while I shall be teenage and soon after that I will be a man. Then I can start to properly plan for my return to Paris. I know Marie is waiting for me. We had a promise; to be friends, to ride ponies over the fields. We will drink champagne together and I will eat lobster. For Marie.

# Villa Marta

---

The sun rose gently over Villa Marta like a little half-baked madeleine but by nine o'clock it was a giant lobster, squeezing the pretty pensión in its red claws. Honeysuckle and rose tumbled over the walls of the Villa. The petals fattened and were forced apart. Dismembered blossom dangled in the probing heat. Sally and Rose stumbled down to the patio and ate their hard rolls called bocadillos, and drank bowls of scummy coffee, feeling faintly sick because of the heat and the coffee. The tables on the terrace had been arranged under a filigree of vine and splashes of sun came through, burning them in patches. Behind a cascade of leaves which made a dividing curtain, a group of Swedish boys watched them with pale, intelligent eyes. 'You come out with us,' they hissed solemnly through the vines; 'you come fucky-fuckies.'

They stretched out beside the pool and talked about food and records and sex appeal and sex. Already they had learned a thing or two. Sally had discovered, from a survey in *Time* magazine, that smoking added fifty per cent more sex appeal to a girl. They wondered if you were hopelessly, truly in love, would you know because you would even think a man's thing was nice looking. This was a mystery and also a risk because if such a love did not exist and you spent your life waiting for it, you would be on the shelf, an old maid and hairy.

Built into their contempt for old maids was the knowledge that marriage meant an end to office life and it was so pleasant to lie by the pool, barely disturbed by the prowling vigil of the Swedish boys and the sun rolling over them in bales of heat, that both were intent on a domestic resolution.

It was merely a question of finding the right man or finding the right feelings for some sort of man. When they spoke of their married lives, Sally detailed a red sofa and Japanese paper lanterns. Rose was going to have a television in the bedroom.

Sometimes they fetched a guitar and went and sat among the cacti and sang; 'Sally free and easy, that should be her name – took a sailor's loving for a nursery game.'

In the afternoons, they went for a walk around the streets of Palma. Sally wore a dress of turquoise frills. Rose's frock was white linen. It was the era of the minis but they turned up the hems several times over so that the twitch of their buttocks showed a glimpse of flower-patterned panty. Men followed them up and down the hot, narrow lanes. 'See how they look at you!' Sally shuddered. 'Their eyes go down and up as if they can look right inside you.'

'Why would they want to do that?' Rose said.

In fact she was very aware of their pursuers, of the tense silence in the street behind them as if the air itself was choked with excitement – the stalking whisper of plim-solled feet on cobbles – the hot, shocked breath on the back of the neck. One day one of them captured her as she rounded a corner, caught her by the waist with a hand as brown as a glove and gazed into her face with puzzled eyes and then he kissed her. She slapped his face and ran on giggling to catch up with her friend but all day little fingers of excitement crept up and twisted inside her.

In the evenings they grew despondent for the heat of the day made them lethargic and they did not enjoy the foreign food. 'Drunk-man's-vomit-on-a-Saturday-night,' Sally would sigh, spooning through a thick yellow bean soup.

After dinner there began a long ritual of preparation, of painting eyes and nails, of pinning little flowers and jewelled clips in their hair before going out dancing. They did not bother much with washing because they had dipped in the pool during the day and the showers at the Villa Marta were violent and boiling, but they sprayed recklessly with *L'Air du Temps*.

The dances were not, actually, fun. The boys were young and eager but their desire was not skilfully mounted. They yapped and scrabbled like puppies. They did not know how to make sex without touching so that it hung in heavy droplets on the air. They did not know how to make fire from sticks.

One day on the beach they met a group of Americans, schoolgirls from a convent in Valencia, tall and beautiful although they were only fifteen. They had come to the island for a holiday and the girls pitied them because they still seemed bound by school regulations, crunching the white-hot sand in leather shoes that were the colour of dried blood. The shoes were only taken off when they went into the water and tried to drown one of their companions. The girls joined in splashing the victim who was blonde and tanned and identical in appearance to the others, until they realised that she was terrified and in genuine danger of drowning. 'Stop!' Sally commanded nervously. 'She's afraid!'

'She's a creep,' one of the pretty girls said.

'Why?' Rose pulled the sodden beauty from the floor of the ocean.

'*She* hasn't got oxblood loafers.'

A few days later the Americans came running along the beach, their heavy golden hair bouncing, their feet like aubergines in the shiny purple shoes. 'Hey!' they called out to Rose and Sally who were bathing grittily in the sand. 'There's sailors.'

An American ship had docked in Palma. The girls watched silently as the sailors were strewn along the quay, wonderful in uniforms that were crisp as money. They whistled at the girls and the girls ran after them, their knees shivering on the sweet seductive note. 'Come on, honey,' one boy called to them. 'Where d'you wanna go? You wanna go to a bullfight?' 'Sure!' the American girls agreed, and their leather shoes squeaked and their rumps muscled prettily under little shorts as they ran to catch up.

Sally and Rose had been hoping for something more attractive than a bullfight. Given the opportunity they might have pressed for lunch in one of the glass-fronted restaurants in Palma, where lobsters and pineapples were displayed in the window; but the Americans moved in a tide, scrambling for a bus, juggling with coins and they had to run or get left behind.

Following the example of the giant schoolgirls they pressed themselves down beside the loose forms of two of the young men. 'I'm Will,' the boy beside Sally said, showing wonderful teeth and something small and grey and lumpy like a tiny sheep, which was endlessly ground between them. 'I'm Bob,' Rose's sailor said and laughed to show that names were not to be taken seriously.

The bullring smelled like a cardboard box that had got damp and been left to dry in the sun. It was constructed as a circus with benches arranged in circles on different levels and all of those spaces were crammed with human beings who were waiting for a death. They were pungent with heat and the tension of expectation.

This dire harmony wrought a huge hot communal breath which had a little echo in the men who had followed the girls through the lanes of Palma, but here the fear was not exciting and pleasant. Sally and Rose did not believe in death. They sat clammy with dismay, waiting for the animals to be saved.

No matter that it was an honourable sport, that the dead bulls' meat fed the island's orphans; they were unimpressed by the series of little fancy men who pranced around the bewildered animals which lurched and pawed at bubbles of their own blood that bulged brilliantly and then shrank back shabbily into the sand.

How many orphans could so small an island support Rose wondered, as one animal died and then two? She saw the orphans as the left luggage of tourists who had stayed too long in the lanes. She sympathized with this; she too had wanted, in an awful way, to go back alone, without Sally. Her only dismay was for the huge animals crumbling down one by one with hot dribbles and their sides all lacquered red by a pile of little sticks jammed in like knitting needles stuck in a ball of wool.

'He's dead!' Sally accused Will. A third animal folded up its slender legs and rolled in the sticky sawdust.

'Sure is honey,' Will said eagerly and squeezed her fingers. He seemed radiantly happy. 'Say, can I come on back to your hotel?'

Sally gave Rose a careful look. Rose's sailor, Bob, was watching Will for a clue.

Rose thought it wouldn't matter much what happened to Sally since Sally's period was late following some home-based encounter. She calculated some basis on which to make it worthwhile for herself. 'We're late for our dinner,' she said. 'We'd have to have a hamburger.'

'Sure thing,' Bob said amiably.

The girls ate with the speed and concentration of thieving dogs. Their pocket money did not run to delicacies. The sailors treated them to banana splits and the girls thought they should have ordered prawn cocktails and steaks since these men were so rich and so foolish with their money.

On their way back to the hotel after supper they were wreathed in virtue. It was thick around them, like scent over the honeysuckle. Both of them felt like sacrificial virgins although they were not, actually, virgins. In the terms of the understanding, they were going to lie down beside Will and Bob and let them do, within reason, what they wanted. They walked together, no longer feeling a need to be sociable. The sailors were playful in their wake.

When they got to the hotel they let the men into their room and sat with cold invitation on either bed. The sailors took cigarettes from their pockets and asked if there was anything to drink. Rose grudgingly brought a bottle of Bacardi from the wardrobe. 'I gotta girl like you at home,' Bob said. He rubbed her hand and drew up a linty patch on her burnt skin.

He kissed her then and she could feel his dry lips stretched in a smile even as they sought her mouth. He was the most amiable man she had ever met. She had no notion how to treat or be treated by a man as an equal. Sexual excitement grew out of fear or power. She could only regard him with contempt. 'You like to see my girl?' he said. He brought out his wallet and withdrew some coloured snapshots of a girl with a rounded face and baby curls.

Will had pictures too. Chapters of American life were spread out on the woven bedspreads and soon the girls were lulled into yawns by the multitude of brothers and sisters, moms and dads, *dawgs* and faithful girlfriends.

The sailors spoke of the lives they would have, the houses and children. They had joined the navy to see the world but it seemed that their ship was in a bottle. Soon they would settle down, have families, mow the grass at weekends. The lives ahead of them were as familiar and wholesome as family serials on the television.

Catching Sally's eye, which was hard under the watering of boredom, Rose suddenly suffered an enlightenment. It was herself that she saw in the balding Polaroids – at the barbecue, at the bake sale – squinting into the faded glare of the sky. She was looking at her future.

She gathered in her mind from the assorted periods of films she had seen, a white convertible with a rug and a radio on the back seat, a beach house with a verandah, an orchestra playing round the pool in the moonlight. All Americans had television in the bedroom.

'Bob, put your arms around me,' she said. She swept the photographs into a neat pile and put them prissily face down. Bob's arms fell on her languidly. She drew them back and arranged them with efficiency, one on a breast and one on a hard, brown leg. He gave her a swift look of query but she closed her eyes to avoid it and offered him her open mouth. 'You're as ripe as a little berry. You sure are,' Bob sighed, and for once his smile faded and languor forsook him. He began kissing her in a heavy rhythmic way and his hands pursued the same rhythm on her spine, on her breasts, on her thighs. Rose had a moment of pure panic. She could not think. Her good shrewd plotting mind had deserted her. Clothes, body, common sense seemed to be slipping away and she was fading into his grasp, the touch of his tongue and fingertips, velvety, masterly, liquidy.

She opened her eyes to gaze at him and saw his goodness in the chestnut sweep of his eyebrows and his hair. 'I love you,' was the first thought to return to her head. She reached out to touch his hair.

Bob felt her stillness. He opened his eyes. He found himself staring into blue eyes that were huge with something that he saw as fear. He pushed her away harshly. 'Now don't you go around doing that sort of thing with all the guys,' he said. 'You're a nice girl.'

Rose did not know what to do. Bob shook his head and stood up. He fetched his cigarettes from the dressing table. He tapped the pack on his palm to release one, but he hit it with such violence that all the cigarettes were bent. He lit one anyway and went to the window, opening the shutters and leaning out to sigh long and deeply. Rose, watching the indifferently entwined bodies on the other bed, felt very close to tears.

'Jesus Christmas!' Bob let out a whoop. 'Would you look at that pool!'

In a second, Will had leaped from the disarrayed Sally and joined his friend, his buddy, at the window.

'Holy shit!' Will said with reverence.

'Mind your mouth.' Bob cuffed him good-humouredly. 'Last man in is a holy shit.'

The Villa Marta was constructed on a single storey so the young men were able to let themselves out the window with a soft thump on the cactussy lawn. They breathed muffled swearwords as the cacti grazed their ankles and then ran to the pool, tearing off their beautiful uniforms as they went.

The girls stood at the window watching them playing like small boys in the water. They splashed each other and pulled at one another's shorts. Will jumped from the water, waving his friend's underpants. 'Hey, come back here,' Bob yelled. 'I got a bare ass.'

'Don't worry,' his friend hollered back. 'It's a small thing.'

Bob scrambled from the pool and they tussled on the edge of the prickly lawn. With a cold pang Rose noted that his body was beautiful, every part of it, golden and beautiful. She beat on the shutters savagely with her knuckles. 'You out there! You better go now,' she said.

'Sure thing!' the sailors laughed with soft amusement as they pulled on their clothes.

They came to the window to kiss the girls goodnight and then leaped at the flower-covered wall to scramble on to the street.

'Bob,' Rose howled out softly. Bob dropped back lightly to the ground. He came back to where she was huddled at the window. 'What's up honey?'

'Don't you have a pool at home?' she said. She was troubled by the way he had reacted to the pool at the Villa Marta. All Americans had swimming pools.

'What kind of a question is that?' Bob said. 'We don't have no pool. We live in the hills. We gotta few cows and hens and sheep. We gotta few acres but we ain't got no pool.'

He ran off again but before making his effortless jump at the wall he paused and cried out, 'Wait for me!' and she thought of his chestnut hair and the wild sweetness of his touch and said yes, she would wait, but then she saw the bleak snowfall of blossoms from the wall and she realized that he had been calling out to his buddy. He was gone.

She ran from the room and out into the dark, polish-smelling hall of the Villa. As she stood trying to compose herself, the front door opened and two of the Swedish boys entered. They were immaculately attired in evening dress and carried half-filled bottles of whiskey but both seemed as sober as Mormons.

'Good evening,' one said.

'You like to fuck sailors?' the other enquired respectfully. He had watched the visitors emerging from the wall.

Rose hurled herself at him, slapping his face with both hands in a fury. He delivered his bottle for safe-keeping to his friend and calmly trapped her hands with his. 'You act like the little wolf' – he spoke with detachment – 'but you are really the grandmother in disguise.'

He let her go and she fled through the carved entrance, tearing along the street, down one alley, through the next. She emerged into a long, tree-lined street and there were the sailors. She stood and watched them until the young men had disappeared and only the hipswing of their little buttocks was picked out by the moon like ghostly butterflies in their tight white pants.

'Creeps,' she cried after them.

# The Miracle of Life

I grew up on a street that was skilled in competitive sameness. All the houses boasted a radiant darkness. Pine green or woodstain doors opened to admit or dispatch men in suits, women in costumes, children with long socks and cumbersome frocks and hairy cardigans. The women were constantly afraid that their children would disgrace them in front of the neighbours, the men feared that their wives would let them down by speaking out or earning money and the children worried that no one would know they were unique.

We knew our street had its share of scandals which were much discussed and used as an innoculation against any serious threat of independence. There was Mrs Galvin who ran off with a man and afterwards her small daughter fell out a window. I always pictured the child arched out the frame for a last disbelieving glance, finally toppling as the sinful couple sprinted around the corner. There was Mrs Beech whose husband died and she had to go to work and this so confused her son that he dressed up as a nun. There was Miss Milne-Evans who was a Protestant and a spinster and went mad behind the cobwebby growths that enclosed her big house. Always it was the women. Men's only flaw was failure – failure to make their name or to combat death or keep their hands off the bottle or the women.

I worried about our mother. For instance, although

she never went out without her cherry-coloured high heels and her grey two-piece, there was a line of clothes across the kitchen to air and we often ate eccentric meals, tinned sardines with creamed potatoes or curried eggs.

She was respectful to my father but she said heretical things. While she savagely tackled housework in our gloomy kitchen, where light never entered but remained a wistful onlooker at the one small window, she declared that girls were as good as boys, that sex was no picnic, that the key to a woman's happiness was her own income.

One day she told me the facts of life. She drew sperms on a paper grocery bag and concocted a tale so improbable, so far removed from suits and costumes and fathers and mothers that I knew I could no longer trust her. The telling gave her a hectic energy and she went off to scrub the floor, leaving me to look at the bag of human commas. When the red had receded from her face she made tea and grew sentimental. She said the baby that got born was one of millions of sperms that ran in a race until it reached the safety of the womb. She called it the miracle of life.

Awful, I called it. I believed that I had come from somewhere special; I imagined I had been spirited to my mother's body as a sort of fairy doll.

Afterwards I took a bus into D'Olier Street and stood for a long time at the window of the Gas Company Showrooms looking at the model refrigerator. Food was displayed on its shelves, sausages and ham, a roast chicken, a trifle, a bunch of bananas, a whole cheese. It was not real food. It was made of papier mâché and had a dry and itchy look. I liked it because it was both orderly and exotic. It was part of a new world which ought to be my inheritance. In 1960, apart from Elvis Presley singing 'Old Shep', it was my favourite thing in the world.

It was close to Christmas and ropes of fairy lights swooped over O'Connell Street and the shawlies of Moore Street shouted: 'Penny the sparklers.' I no longer cared for all that. The glitter gave me an uneasy memory of Reenee as she had been. Besides, I was not, any more, a child.

Children grow up in secret. They choose their models from the random assortment of people in their path. We did not have a television, which provides the ideals of fantasy for today's children, nor any modern appliance except a vacuum cleaner the size of a St Bernard dog which sometimes spat fire from its hoses. Parents were used only as models for avoidance. I loved my mother and I stuck close to her, drinking tea and eating Hovis in the kitchen after school, but it seemed vital to turn into a different person. I had flung out a schizophrenic net to cover, at the calm end of the pond, our nun, Sister Sophie, and at its deepest and most dangerous extreme, my best friend Katie's older sister, Reenee.

Katie and I had been Reenee's handmaidens. We ran her bath (one keeping a hand in the water until the temperature was exactly right), backcombed her hair, painted her nails. At least once a week we were party to dramatic scenes such as the following:

Reenee was getting ready for a dance. From her bedroom she sent out a thin shriek, summoning Katie and me. 'For God's sake, I've got a spot!'

She was in her half slip and orangey-tan nylons, her sweater flung on the bed, her breasts overflowing the rigid cones of her bra. Her blue satin dress with the tulip skirt and cut-out back was hanging on a chair. We ran about like blind mice, trying to appease her, trying to discern the flaw.

'On my back, for Christ's sake,' Reenee snapped and we found it and it was quite a big spot too.

Katie boiled a kettle and fetched cotton wool and disinfectant and Reenee's Pan-Stik make-up. I got a darning needle and poised it over a jet of flame on the gas cooker. When the needle was red hot I poked it at the centre of the spot and Katie dabbed at its erupting substance. '*Don't* squeeze!' Reenee warned. She began to calm down as we patted in the orangey emulsion that matched her stockings better than her skin. At this stage her eyes narrowed with satisfaction at her reflection in the winged dressing-table mirror and she told us the things she knew. S.A. was what made a woman ir-resistible. You got it by putting pads of cotton wool, soaked in perfume, in your bra. No girl should go all the way but it was all right above the waist if you were going steady. A married woman must always keep her lipstick and mascara beneath the pillow and put them on before her husband awoke so that he would never have to look on her naked face. She spoke of French kissing, of lurching, of *shifting*.

We knew about French kissing, for it was the fate of all women who were brought to the pictures by their boyfriends. Reenee said it was lousy unless you were crazy about the guy and then it was fab. Lurching was close dancing and an occasion of sin. We never quite found out what shifting was but it concerned couples who rolled about the floor at parties.

We watched Reenee like a hawk. She knew all the rules of life and was confident in their execution. When she spoke on the telephone to her boyfriend, Tom, she leaned back in the chair and stretched out a leg and dangled her shoe. She smiled and made sheep's eyes into the telephone.

We both thought that it was the oddest thing, to

smile into that handle of black Bakelite, but we made a mental note of it.

Sister Sophie was entirely different, a pious little stick of a woman who told us of a girl who had dressed up in her brother's clothes on Hallowe'en and afterwards she died and her parents saw her ghost, still dressed in men's clothing, flapping about in the moon. She thought I was a good child and prayed constantly for my vocation. I was not drawn to the nuns' way of life, their gliding blackness and the dull certainty of their salvation, but so far she was the only one who had noticed anything about me.

That year two things happened. The first was that Reenee got a crippling disease. In the beginning it crept up slowly like a bad 'flu and she maintained her glamour, propped up in bed in fluffy layers of her favourite blue. Then all of a sudden, she was an invalid, yellow and shapeless and sour and stale. The mysterious womanly parts of her that had been such a source of envy and admiration to us now became the necessity for odious tasks which Katie, blazing with hatred, had to perform. I was no longer involved; I did not have to be so I retreated. Neither of us felt sorry for her. We considered that she had let us down and we despised her. Katie had to share a room with her, with all that soft, sad, dying femaleness. Sometimes when I walked to school with her I could smell Reenee's smell from her and I imagined her pale, intense face had a yellowish tinge. I thought that Reenee's illness would spread and spread like St Brigid's cloak until it covered us all, so I took to going into school early on my own to help Sister Sophie with her dahlias and I stayed on late, when lessons were over, to polish the blackboard and the desks.

I told Sister Sophie I had got The Call. The nun smuggled in special treats for me, Taylor Keith lemonade, Mikado biscuits, iced fairy cakes from the Eaton. She talked about God. She made Him sound like a brother, impractical and all-powerful. I liked that because I only had sisters, but the cakes caught in my throat.

The second thing to happen was that Betty Malibu came to live on our street. Her real name was Mrs Cahill but she told Mrs Elliot next door that she had once sung in the Gaiety as Betty Malibu and after that the name stuck. She was tall and thin with a mock ocelot coat and blonde hair in long waves. She had a husband, Barney, never seen except as a cigar pointing at the windscreen of a Mercedes car. She herself had a car – an unheard of thing for a housewife – a blue Ford Zephyr, which sometimes made snorting sorties down the street, almost killing people. Most of the time she preferred to walk, pushing a go-car to show off her little girl who was called Lucille and who struggled within a pyramid of pink nylon frills. Sometimes when she walked her daughter, she sang to her. I thought she was like Grace Kelly. She was the most admirable woman I had ever seen.

The other women did not like her. They said her American accent had come out of a packet of Mary Baker cake mix. They laughed when she said she put pineapple pieces in her ice cubes. They said that she had come from nothing.

When she was new on the street they tried to impress her. One told her how she had done all her curtains that day because there was a good breeze and another said that she had finished her whole batch of Christmas baking. A third one had cleaned out all her presses to make way for her new cauliflower pickle.

Betty Malibu smiled her dreamy smile. 'I did bugger all,' she said.

Nothing could reduce her in my eyes. If she had come from nothing, then what a remarkable journey she had made, to bring such glamour to our street. She always seemed dressed for a party. I thought the pineapple pieces in the ice cubes sounded so smart, and they meant she had a refrigerator too.

When I said this to my mother, when I praised her mock ocelot coat and her blue car and her gold hair, Mother turned from her polishing with an angry look and said: 'If you think she's got more to offer than we have, why don't you just take yourself over there?'

I did. I put on my pink coat, handed down by a richer cousin, and went and knocked on our new neighbour's door. She was wearing a nylon housecoat with frills. She apologized for it, calling it a peignoir.

'Can I come in and play?'

She gave a little yawn. I think she had been having a nap. 'Who are you?'

'I live down the road.'

'Sure. Come in, little girl. Would you like to watch some television?'

'I'd like to see your refrigerator,' I said.

There was a pause. 'Sure, honey.' She led me through the house which was full of glittering ornaments and bright pieces of china, like the prizes on a raffle stall. 'Would you like to do a job for me while you're in the kitchen? I'll give you a Bounty Bar.'

The 'fridge was in the kitchenette, where it took up most of the space. It was both tall and squat and every so often it seemed to give a deep chuckle. I drew back its vaulty door. The cold light inside, the white interior, the rows of ribbed shelves like bars on a coat, reminded me of a hospital ward. There was no trifle. No ham or bananas. There was hardly any food there at all, just some plastic boxes and greaseproof bags and a lettuce squashed under a stippled plastic shelf at the bottom. I frowned into the chill emptiness.

'What's the matter, honey? Did you want a sand-wich?'

'There's nothing in there.'

'Sure there is. It's in the bags,' she said. 'You have to cover the food in a 'fridge or else you get odour.' She wanted me to clean out a chicken. 'My stomach just turns over,' she sighed.

Disappointment lay like a stone on my heart but I clawed chicken guts out on to newspaper. I would never do this for my mother. 'What about the pineapple ice cubes?' I said very quietly.

'Oh, sweet! – They're just for parties.'

'Don't you make ice-pops or ice-cream in the 'fridge?'

'No,' she agreed amiably. 'But we will someday if you want.'

I forgave her. She made coffee – not Irel, which we drank at home, but proper Nescafé. She gave me a Mars Bar and a Bounty. These were English and we could not buy them.

I came to see her every day. I told my mother I was going to Katie's house and, forsaking the dahlias, led Sister Sophie to believe that my mother wanted me (which was not exactly a lie, but did not merit the specific truth I gave it). Betty Malibu and I sat in her drawing room, which had a red carpet and satinized wallpaper, and watched Armand and Michaela Denis wrestling with blurred black and white lions. When we were not watching television we talked about the stars. She bought all the movie magazines and knew about the personal life of every actor and actress: *Bobby and Sandra's Marriage Crisis! Has Eddie Left Debbie Holding the Baby? Janet and Tony – Together Again?* I learned from these publications that having a bosom was the true secret of S.A. and indeed the root of every female success. At the

back of the magazines were advertisements for wigs and
false bosoms and even false bottoms so that having
savoured the turbulent personal lives of the stars you
could send off your cheque (or check, as they called it)
and receive in the post a parcel of parts which made you
just like the screen goddesses.

I felt at my chest and found that two small softnesses
covered the wings of bone. I developed a great longing.
'There's just one thing I want for Christmas,' I confided
to Betty Malibu, the only person in the world to whom
I could say such a thing. She laughed when I told her.
'Well, that doesn't sound too difficult.'

But it was. Nobody ever bought you the things you
wanted and they never liked the things you gave them.
If I told the family I wanted a bra for Christmas they
would laugh at me and say: 'What are you going to put
in it – your scapulars?'

Apart from my new craving I loved books. I knew
this addiction to be a dowdy one but still I bought
books for everyone at gift-giving times.

I spent hours crawling around the floor under the
bargain table in Fred Hannas, where nothing cost more
than sixpence. I bought adventure stories for my sisters,
an old cookery book for my mother; for Father I found
a volume called *Sailing up the Belgian Congo*. As an
afterthought I picked up a book of faded photographs
about a tame bear for Katie. There was nothing good
enough for Betty Malibu. All my usual pleasure at book
hunting turned to panic as I flung aside old Protestant
Bibles and street directories, tomes of Dickens and Chau-
cer, smelling of mould.

It was while I was there, under the table with the
unwanted Greats, that Reenee, crying out a lament
about a hangnail, summoned Katie to her side and died.

The funeral was four days before Christmas. Everyone

was there, full of regret and chilled by the nudge of mortality. Katie and her mother cried and cried until they seemed to dry out and I was crying too but my misery had a different source.

At school the day before, Sister Sophie had given me a mission. One of the bold girls in the class – an Audrey or an Alma or Dolores – (good girls were always Josie or Brid or Teresa) had been found with an object of obscenity hidden in her desk. That's what Sister Sophie called it. She held up a bulky grey cardboard folder. Concerning its contents, she said, she would leave our innocence undisturbed. All that remained was to dispose of the dirty work and she would give this task to a good child whom she could trust. I stepped forward without being asked. She put the book in my hands.

'Promise you won't look,' she said.

'I swear.'

I did not look – not really look – but as the folder slipped into the waste bin its pages parted and my eye was drawn to the flickering show of Hollywood stars. It was a home-made film album, not just with magazine cut-outs but proper glossy photographs of the kind that fan clubs supply. Before I could think my hands had plunged into the dank cavern of refuse and the album was safe in my grasp. It had suffered only a little in the bin and a quick peek assured me that Alma or Dolores had not identified ownership with the usual: 'This book belongs to . . .' I could feel my heart juddering like an old motor engine as I ran back into school and hid the album in the cloakroom, underneath my overcoat.

I brought Betty Malibu her present after school, wrapped up in a sheet of shop wrapping paper, which cost twopence. She was as excited as I was. 'Oh, you sweet child, wait till I tell them all that you went to the trouble of getting me a Christmas present.' I was pulling ribbons away from the box she had given me – too big for a bra alone so I knew there must be other things as well and I kept my fingers crossed for a stiff slip and nylons.

It was a dress – pink Vyella with blue and green smocking on its flat, flat chest. It was what my mother would call a good item, with spare buttons on a card and little loops inside the shoulders to keep your slip straps in place. I recognized it from an expensive children's shop called The Gay Child.

'Isn't that the cutest thing, honey?' Betty Malibu was delighted. 'I chose it specially to go with your pink coat. Won't you be the smartest kid on the street?'

I nodded bitterly. That was just what I would be.

She was still smiling as she tore the wrapping from her gift. When the folder was revealed she got a puzzled look. She flipped through it and I saw that her fingers were as stiff as Sister Sophie's when she had held it up in class. 'Hey!' She gave a funny little laugh. 'What is this?'

'It's your present.'

When I looked at her she had withdrawn from the album and sat quite still, tears gathering in her eyes. 'Is this what you call a joke?' She said it very softly. 'It's not even new. It's garbage. It's *dirty*!' Her shining nails brushed a scar of grease which clung to the cover where it had been dipped in the bin. 'I thought you were getting me a book. I thought you were buying me a new book.'

'I didn't think you'd read a book,' I protested. 'You were going to buy me a bra.'

'You shouldn't judge a person by where they come from,' she said with intense feeling. 'I thought you would have something written on the inside and I would show everyone how you had bought me a book and written in it for me. A bra!' She pulled the rags of the wrapping paper around the gift for decency. 'What would your mother say?'

After Reenee's funeral service the mourners seemed drawn by a need for comfort to the Christmas crib, with its real straw and its nice little plaster donkey.

There had been hymns and inspiring passages of scripture and these helped to wipe away the yellowness of Reenee's illness. We all saw her as she had been, blonde and backcombed and full of S.A., but now with the addition of her heavenly crown, like a seaside beauty queen. In the end it seemed that she had simply got bored with us and gone off to look for more exciting company. It made us sad. We thought we would never laugh again. Then Betty Malibu leaned into the crib and looked at the baby Jesus with interest. 'It just goes to show,' she said; 'you should never judge a person by where they start out from.' Everyone gave a little titter.

My mother made me wear the pink dress on Christmas day. She inspected all the seams and fancy stitches and marvelled at the good taste of a person like Betty Malibu. A funny thing had happened. Mother called around to the house to thank her for the gift and after that she couldn't stop saying what a nice person she really was and how clean her house was and in a day or two all the neighbours were flocking around Betty Malibu and they even began calling her plain old Mrs Cahill. I didn't care any more. I was feeling so rotten I didn't even mind putting on the dress. If someone had told me to, I would have dressed up in the back half of a pantomime horse. All the books I had bought and disguised with pads of newspaper underneath the wrapping ended up as more signposts to my oddness. 'We know!' my sisters teased as I arranged the nicely bumpy packages beneath the Christmas tree. 'They're only old books, aren't they?'

I took the dress out of its box and looked in misery on its neat round collar, the tweaking puffs of the sleeves. I pulled it over my head and felt behind my neck to slide the buttons into their perfect holes. After a long time I looked.

What I saw was something remarkable. The dress did not change me. Wearing it did not turn me into a kid. It did not alter me at all. Inside it, I was still me, a girl with thin plaits and a heart-shaped face on which intelligence sat like a blight, like spectacles; with the beginnings of a bust showing determinedly beneath the flattening bands of smocking.

If it was so, if a child's dress could not turn me into a child, then a bra or a false bust or even a false bottom could not turn me into a woman. I was uniquely myself and the only one of my kind. I had swum in a race with millions but I was the one who had won the race. I could learn from the experience of others without having to share the perils of their fate. My life was mine, whether I learned to smile at the telephone or sing to my children like Grace Kelly, with or without S.A.

'Look at her!' my sisters jeered when I sat down to dinner in the dress. 'Who does she think she is?' My father looked up from his carving with that vague dismay that love of daughters meant. His eye registered my new dress, or something that it suggested. 'She needs a bra!' he told my mother crossly and then went back with relief to his virtuoso solo upon the Christmas turkey.

# A Particular Calling

In the window of Dooley's Bar a black Morris Minor slid behind the crusted gold lettering of a misted mirror past an acrobatic display of whiskey bottles filled with something palely whiskey-tinged, some dyed formaldehyde. 'Nice cup of tea,' the driver said kindly and the car sailed into a wide main street which was pressed down by grey sky and lined on cither side with grey buildings stubbily imprinted with shops, emporia and licensed premises of a uniform nursery dullness.

The place had the preserved look of a museum. Outflung overalls and silent boots in Carbury's Drapery suggested the remnants of a tribe more than the treat of a new cardigan or a little Communion frock for a child. There was nothing for a young girl to look at – no Ballet Bra, seven and elevenpence, or Bradmola stockings tinted like the skin of Red Indians. In the glass front of the Dainty Bakery the big hard-looking cakes of bread and currant loaves had settled into the sullen permanence of sleeping cats. A cactus plant licked a gilt-framed Our Lady of Perpetual Succour with faded, saw-tooth tongues, in among the Milk of Magnesia bottles and tins of sheep dip in Markey's Pharmacy. There was hardly anyone in the street. A few women with empty message bags and a man on a bicycle moved in dislocated isolation, like refugees.

A child ran across the road chewing a stalk of rhubarb

and the woman waved, but the girl stepped back and stared as if there was something of which a stranger ought to have been warned. Even the piles of cow dung, heaped up randomly in the road, some flattened by tractor wheels or bleeding thickly into puddles, had a look of old occupation.

'Well, here we are!' The woman brought her Morris Minor to a halt outside the largest of the grey buildings which was Sinnott's Commercial and was a hotel. As she lifted out her cases and stood in the street to refresh herself with the town's odd stout and manure breath, there was a tumult of bells. Hundreds of people were coming towards her. She remained on the dirty pavement, half smiling, her pink face and Toni-waved hair imperturbable as the horde advanced. The bells continued to clang as more people streamed through tall silver gates, the women all in hats and headscarves. 'Oh, it's a Holy Day,' the woman laughed in relief. She had developed a habit of speaking kindly to herself, or bracingly. 'Everyone was at Mass.' She was not a Catholic but had made this difference as discreet as possible and prided herself that she fitted in. She went into the hotel and was shown up to her room with its stained pink quilt and empty fireplace, the wallpaper patterned with sepia stains. 'Very nice. Thank you,' she said.

While she waited for tea and a Polo biscuit she wrote out two cards.

'Miss Patricia Higgins is in Sinnott's Hotel from Tuesday 14th to Friday 17th for the usual services.' She went out again to pin one of these in the porch of the now-deserted church and she left the second on the noticeboard in the hotel foyer. As she savoured the flesh-coloured cup of tea and biscuit exotically zested with coconut, she laid out her things – her own lamp which counteracted the unsavoury effect of the little plastic shade, a clean white sheet with which to cover the queasy duvet, her black box with its secrets.

Sometimes she was asked if she was lonely. The nature of her work kept her in contact with one sex only and meant she couldn't mix socially with the other. Her clients did not like it known that they visited her, or for what purpose, so she stayed away from the hotel's lounge bar and the cinema and ate alone, mostly in her room but an odd time she came down to the dining room and was shown to one of those peculiar corner tables that are saved for the solitary, imprisoning the diner into a recess in distant view of celebrant groups and couples. On these occasions she forced herself to concentrate on the food in some abstract manner; trying, for instance, to think of words that would rhyme with liver – river, shiver, deliver, giver, quiver.

'Fat chance of lonely,' she laughed at herself. She was a confidante to her clients. When she heard the troubles of married people she could only count her blessings.

Young people with nothing on their minds were even more anxious. When their dreams failed to materialize they themselves grew insubstantial. They needed her, begged her to hurry back. Some of them liked her.

She used to work in Dublin where she lived with her mother. Discretion had no currency in the big city. She did not have to work from a hotel but had a small office close to Camden Street. She had no shortage of callers. One of them came all the way from Mallow in County Cork and had told her that there was a desperate need for her work in the provinces. Such a service was unheard of in rural parts and might be seen as a contravention of nature. People's lives were damaged by its absence. She took her Morris Minor on the road. At first it had been difficult making contact but those who needed her found her. She was overwhelmed with business.

Sometimes she could not get home to spend the weekend with her mother.

She had her pets, certain young people with whom there was more than a business affinity. She called them her dotes and bucked up their confidence. Country life could be cruel to the young. Parents were strict and there wasn't a lot in the way of social life. They saved up for her the diaries of their hopes and talked of true love and happiness as if it was a harvest that merely had to come ripe and could be plucked off in the hand.

A week from now she would be seeing her best pet who was waiting for her by the sea. She should have been there two months past but was kept at home by her mother's illness. 'Only a week!' she beamed and dragged her mind away from the smug look on her mother's face as the doctor declared her dead.

She liked the seaside. People were friendly and used to strangers. She could walk on the beach and smoke her cigarettes and mingle with the holiday revellers, the children dancing in the waves in their knickers. She did not favour the flat towns of the midland. It was only duty that brought her to this part of the country. Midland was cattle country. The men in the hotels were purple-faced fellows. The rooms were without comfort, designed for men, with bits of lino on the floor and yellow lighting that showed up the sheets an un-wholesome colour. She did not sleep well for the hotels were in the main street which at night attracted snorting cars and motorbikes, unseen by day. She had to listen to the sounds of men answering the call of nature against the hotel's facade or hold herself rigid against the violence of men being ill in the street when they had visited the chip shop after the pub was closed. It affected her with nausea. Her own digestion, when she stayed in such places, was made uneasy by menus featuring huge fatty steaks and coarse grills. There was rarely chicken or a ham salad, no sponge cake or dainties.

'Don't you miss having just the one person of your own?' her pet often asked her. 'I have my mother,' she used to say. Her placid eyes filled up but she reminded herself of the success of her business, the satisfaction of her work. Never a minute to herself. She had only time to stand on a chair and pluck from the light cord a strip of sticky paper where flies lay dying and there was a knock on the door.

It was a new client, young and shy with timid eyes and a sparse orange moustache. Patricia Higgins put out a plump hand. 'You're very welcome, indeed you are. Come in and make yourself comfy on the bed.' Still the novice clung to the door and gazed around the challenging decor of the room. 'Does it hurt much?' she said.

When she was first qualified, the travelling electrolysis lady was surprised by the quantity of hair on other women's bodies. She had hardly any body hair. Under her clothes her skin was smooth and cool as marble, as pale as a grey pearl. Her breasts were parchment pale and rather flat but wide in circumference, like saucers of cream. It was not a beautiful body, but it was flawless. In bed she liked to think of those cool unblemished curves beneath her nightie as a temple for the Holy Ghost.

She was an expert at her business. She caused hardly any pain. As she executed unwanted hair roots or cauterized bloody veins she kept up mild conversation. She hardly ever talked about herself.

'You're an intellectual type, aren't you? I said that to myself. I admire a person who can get to grips with books.' She rooted out the orange moustache. She had said that because the girl was plain and would have no romantic secrets to divulge but most likely kept her tufted lip in a book. The girl talked about Karl Marx and Simone de Beauvoir. Miss Higgins said she liked Ngaio Marsh. When the work was finished the girl went and looked at herself in a small piece of mirror that was nailed up over the wash-basin. She ran her fingers over the newly smooth patch above her narrow lips. 'Will it grow again?'

'It does, yes,' Miss Higgins said, 'but you won't have to worry for a long time.'

'Will you come back?' the girl said.

'I keep track of all my clients. I'll be back in time,' she promised. 'Can I have your name for my book?'

'Natasha,' the girl said. 'Natasha Galvin.' She paid Miss Higgins and went to the door where she clung on again, picking at the paint. 'I went to a party,' she said. 'The boys called me Moustasha.' It sounded funny but the poor girl had the look of a cowboy in the pictures when he has just been shot. 'Oh, now love,' Miss Higgins said. 'All that's over. It's just a little thing women sometimes have to cope with.'

She had heard it all before, the cruelty of both sexes towards a woman who failed to meet the standards of grace and beauty. A city woman could be any way, with hair on her face and a baldy head, with warts or no chest and the experts were on hand to remodel her, to curl or straighten, to bleach or paint. Any city girl could be a beauty. A man never knew what he was getting. In the country you were what you were, as God had made you, as they wryly judged. Women whom God had made in vacant mood had to marry an old fellow, half blind, or live at home with the pigs and their father or bury themselves in a convent. 'Sticks and stones,' she tried to remind hurt young women, but the insults were something worse, more akin to boiling oil. Beardy Bridie, Tarzan the Ape Man, Hairy Mary. Just for a small natural abundance a woman could be shunned liked a leper. Only Miss Higgins understood. It was a particular calling.

Her special pet was called Maoliosa Quilligan – known as Maisie – but Miss Higgins thought of her as the doe. She had a doe's eyes, huge and melting brown and softly curling brown hair, although she did not have the nature of a doe. She was bold and full of fun. She had the eye of a fellow called Malachy Boland. He had taken her home several times from dances. The doe said he was a wild bucko, but she was stone crazy about him. 'Oh, Miss Higgins, what must it be like to fall into a fellow's arms and let him go on as long as you'd like? I'd give it a go, only if you make them hang on they marry you to put themselves out of their misery.'

Unknown to Malachy Boland she had a natural disposition to a growth of fuzz along the sides of her face and on her neck. When she was ten years married, she said, she'd let it grow anyway, for either Malachy would be so used to her by then he wouldn't notice, or he'd have grown tired of her and wouldn't care.

'Never fear, pet, he'll be sweet on you,' Miss Higgins said. She often brought a small gift for the doe, a box of turkish delight or black grapes from the city because she knew a fellow like Malachy Boland would only court her with his arms and she wanted her to have the niceties. She criticized herself for having favourites. Everyone was equal in the sight of God. She knew that as she understood that her confidential witness was a privilege which commanded impartiality. All the same her pity was directed to the young. She couldn't see why older women bothered, unless it was a disfigurement of the face such as purple veins or a bunch of coarse hairs on the chain. She disapproved of plain vanity and had been made aware of other more complex motives. The women could say anything to her because she had no business with the men.

She was worn out, that first day in the midlands. Sitting down alone to a high tea of a slice of ham with half a tomato and a scallion she was visited by grief. She felt her mother's shadow passing over her, passing on. There was only one other person in the dining room, a commercial traveller with the grey complexion of habitual hotel eating, but she did not want him to see. She bent her head to pour a pool of salad cream on her plate. She had grown used to unburdening herself to her mother, who was herself bound to secrecy, being housebound, who never judged but poured the tea and sliced the Fuller's walnut cake. 'Well, it takes all types,' she would soothingly affirm as Patricia bit into the crumbly icing and spoke of the cruelty to the young, or of some middle-aged woman in whom perfection was newly necessitated by a turn her life had taken.

She managed the ham but left the scallion and went outside to her Morris Minor. She wanted to get away from the town. She drove past the tall grey church, past lime-green fields perpetually consumed by dappled cows, past a big concrete cube in a bog of mud that was called The Allanah Ballroom. She parked the car beside a stream. In its dying moments the sun had crept into the grey sky and appeared as a buttery band on the flat horizon. The air felt nice as she walked along the squelchy grass by the water. Her cigarette smoke dangled on the windless yellow dusk.

She understood that it took all types but she was made a party to the types of lives they led. She was once visited by a widow who needed a little beard removed in order to get a job as a waitress. Miss Higgins did her chin free of charge and said she could pay her the next time, when she had wages. 'You are a dear soul,' the widow told her.

Women like Mrs Manning would never think of her as a dear soul. They winked at her. They imagined she envied and admired them — that she conspired with them.

'Your work won't go to waste,' Mrs Manning had boasted, walking about without a screed to admire her thighs which were wide and newly smooth. She had come to Miss Higgins with a flowing surfeit of personal hair. She was more than forty and had been married twenty years. In all probability her husband admired this quality in his wife. Her plucked limbs were for someone new.

The stream went into a field. There were no cars or dogs around so she followed it and felt soothed by its whispering. Someone said hello and she waved and plodded on. 'Hello!' the man said again and she paused, plumply smiling, confusion locked up inside her as she realized she was trespassing and the man was not greeting her but summoning her attention.

'Are you all right, there?' It was a polite way of asking her what she was doing.

'Sorry,' she said. 'I'm on your land. Lost in thought!' she giggled.

'You're all right,' he said. 'Finish your walk and enjoy your thoughts.'

He was loose-limbed with bristling hair and a long, thoughtful face. He hadn't the coarseness that came to many men whose business was the death of beasts.

'They weren't really very nice,' Miss Higgins hovered; 'my thoughts.'

'Oh, well then.' He looked around as if seeking something pleasant for her to dwell upon. 'Would you come up to the house for a cup of tea?'

'Oh, no.' She was embarrassed and fell silent.

'No, of course you wouldn't. Her heart went out to

him when she saw that he too was abashed. 'That was an awful thing to say. I'm every way since my mother died.'

Her eyes filled with tears and she smiled. 'Oh, that's too bad,' she said gaily and she hurried back to her car, her heels catching in mud so that she must have looked like a duck.

In bed that night he crowded her mind. Her memory cast about for different angles of him and animated them, putting a cup of tea in his hand, putting his hand on hers. This disturbed her because she had never been foolish. She put it down as a reaction to her mother's death and then was overwhelmed with compassion for his own loss. She wanted to hold his face in her hands.

In the morning she was herself again. She ate toast and drank tea in her room, brightened her lips with her Gala lipstick and spat into her brown mascara, scrubbing a little brush on the muddy patch and then combing colour on her lashes. She could scarcely remember the man's long face. She dabbed Max Factor on her cheeks.

She was glad it was Wednesday. She would be out of the town in two days. Her car would be packed up by the time the men assembled in the hotel dining room to eat a big breakfast before market day. Coaxing her car through the jam of cattle left bellowing in the street, she would be on her way to the seaside and the doe with a little gift of Lemons' Pure Sweets.

Lips and loins and throats and ears. She applied herself with deft detachment to the parts most usually associated with love, tenderly removing hormonal surfeit while the women faintly groaned and murmured on about the pains of life. Some were long-standing customers and she had years of family history for reference. Some reproached her for her late arrival and had bristly growths arising from the use of razors. She didn't tell them about her mother. She preferred them to think that she was still in the cosy flat in Dublin, waiting with the Fuller's cake.

That evening she drove out again. She stopped by the stream, since it was a place she knew. She walked for an hour until turned back by a starry sky.

In bed she dreamed of the man. He sat beside her on a bench and she offered him a sandwich from a greaseproof parcel. He took the sandwich and called her a dear soul.

She ate her dinner in the dining room next day. Without his mother, he might eat in a hotel. 'Tick or tin?' the waitress demanded. 'Thin, please,' Miss Higgins requested, understanding that the girl referred to a choice of soups in varying textures. The waitress ignored her preference and brought her a thick pink fluid and white sliced pan. Some farmers came in and ate noisily, drinking beer and pots of tea. Miss Higgins tried not to glance at the door but concentrated on her soup (tomato – mulatto, staccato, gateau, plateau, chateau). When her mutton and mashed turnip came she could not eat it, but asked for the jelly and custard and a cup of tea, scolding herself for waste.

She stood by the stream in the lime-green field and gazed all around her. She could not even see a farm that might be his. She wanted to cry out – help me! Oh, imagine if she did and he appeared. She would smile and say she'd caught her heel but she was all right now, and off she'd scuttle.

On Friday morning she was packed by half past nine. The relief was enormous. She knew now how other women felt when they talked of love, the woolly bondage that pricked and nagged and soured sleep; the craving for something which, when you looked at it closely, was nothing at all.

She longed for the bracing air of the sea, the bold,

harmless intimacies and laughter of the doe. Opening the door of the Morris Minor, she glanced around in pity at the poor cattle, already helplessly besmirching the street.

'Hello,' he said.

'Oh, hello.' She beamed at him mildly, her heart clanging. Of course he was a farmer. Because he looked gentle she had not associated him with the brutal commerce of the market. Now she could feast her eyes, could see to her immense satisfaction that she had not made him up. His eyes were green. He had a weathered bit of tan. His shoes were clean. 'You're not leaving?' he said.

'Oh, no,' she laughed. 'Not till tomorrow.'

'Have a bit of dinner with me,' he said. 'Don't be offended now. You will, won't you?'

'Thank you very much,' she said. 'Well, I must be going for now. About one o'clock, then.' She went back into the hotel to book her room again. She had finished her business in the town. She could go to the pictures with him in the evening, if he liked.

They ate a dreadful meal of boiled fish, its warped bones poking through a clout of sauce. It had to be fish because it was Friday.

The smell of cattle came in from the street and the cheap dining-room furniture was imperilled by the restless bulk and noise of farmers. 'I can't hear my ears,' Miss Higgins smiled. 'I'd take you away from here only I have business,' said the man who was called Tommy Kearney.

'Come up to my room,' she said, her eyes blinking in calm horror as it was said. She couldn't say anything about them not getting up to anything − not without sounding cheap. She couldn't say such things anyway. The stairs were in view of the dining room and her ears burned as they ascended together, imagining the eyes of farmers on her plump navy blue behind.

He sat on the pink quilt. 'You should have nicer than this,' he looked around. 'My mother's bedroom was very finicky, very refined.'

'I like nice things.' She did not want to sit beside him on the bed but was happy to stand by the fireplace watching him.

'Do you know I love a little garden.' He leaned forward. 'Most of the farmers haven't much use for flowers but all living things are beautiful.'

There was no awkwardness, no threat of assault. He talked about his farm and his mother and how he had once wanted to go to Canada but did not like to leave his mother and now it was too late.

She told him of her own parent's slow departure, and how she still referred everything to her, even though she was dead. Although they remained on opposite sides of the room, a pleasant glow encased them and she understood now how poor people managed to survive if they had someone they were fond of, for one could be contented anywhere, bathed in this glow. It was the other side of love, the safety side, the harbour.

At three o'clock he had to leave for bidding. At the door he took her hand. She would have liked to have a go at kissing him but she did not wish to seem practised. She sat on the bed where he had warmed the quilt and watched the market through her window until the poor beasts had been led away in vans squelching through the muck, except those who remained moaning in the street while their owners got drunk in the hotel's bar. She supposed he had to get drunk in order to kiss her. She did not like men who had taken drink but the kissing was something they needed to get over before they could be a couple. She put on her pink dressing gown and tried to read an Agatha Christie, waiting for the last of the vehicles to pull out of town and the long-faced man to have drunk his courage. The knock came after ten. She heard a sniggery little laugh and something inside her contracted. 'Yes?' she said brightly.

The door opened and they came in. Five drunk farmers descended on her, their eyes veined with pink and glazed over like frightened horses.

'Oh,' she said softly, her insides squealing.

'You first, boyo!' They jostled, exploding into little soprano laughs as they pushed each other forward. One of them stumbled and touched her breast and the others made a hissing sound as if he might have burnt himself.

They were what the young girls would call bowsies, leftover bachelors reeking in neglected clothes, their bodies bloated and mottled from beer. Decent women had long ceased to consider them a prospect. They moved in a pack, seeking incitement, still retaining a wistful faith in the filth against which the church had warned them.

Miss Higgins crawled back against the bed-post and held a pillow to her chest. 'What do you want?'

'The usual services.' A bull-faced man reached for her. As he pulled the pillow from her grasp, his hand caught the front of her night-gown and ripped it off like a sheet of lavatory paper. Five men stared at her bare breasts. They gasped aspirations to Jesus, to the Blessed Virgin.

'It's a service for women.' She turned her head away. She could not close her dressing gown. The bull-faced man held on.

'What service could women want? She's a hoor!' A squat man with shiny lips turned inside out from some defect spat on the lino and took off his belt. 'A city hoor. What way do ye do it in the city?' The others, excited by this talk, laughed and beat their fists on their hands.

'Go away,' she begged.

'You think we aren't good enough,' he flicked his belt at her, grazing her cheek. 'You think we haven't money.' He took out a wad of notes and flung it on the bed. 'Tommy Kearney was good enough.'

Miss Higgins burned. They had seen her going up the stairs with the bristle-haired man. They had wondered about her notice on the wall. Maybe Tommy Kearney had boasted to them of imaginary feats. She knew nothing about him. A good ride. That was the term. She knew how the men talked from the things women said to her. She had thrown away her reputation. She was anything they called her. She remained passive as two men seized her arms and dragged her on to the floor. They were pulling at her clothing, pulling at themselves, a blunt inhuman mass smelling of beer and sweat. She had turned them into this. However bad they were, she had made them worse. 'Oh, Mother, what am I?' she cried out silently.

'A dear soul.' It was not her mother's voice that spoke in her head.

'I'm Tommy Kearney's girlfriend,' she whispered. 'I'm his fiancée.'

She crouched beneath a petrified tableau, silent save for the men's bewildered panting. 'Oh, Jesus Mary and Joseph, miss, we're very sorry.' They fumbled their clothes together and wrapped the edges of her gown around her. They stuffed their money back in their pockets. 'He's a nice fellow, miss, we wish you happiness.' 'Not a word now, men are very foolish when they've taken drink.'

'That's all right,' she said. They tiptoed out of the room leaving her smiling from the floor.

On the way to the seaside she was overtaken by violent bouts of shivering. 'Bit of a chill,' she told herself. Feeling guilty, she treated herself to one of the doe's Lemons' Pure Sweets. She couldn't wait for a bit of sea air, a paddle in the ocean.

She had a nice clean room in Aherne's Holiday Hotel. She kept a watch out the window. She knew the doe would be waiting for her, even two months late. Any minute now she would come darting down the road, her brown hair flying, her dark eyes full of shining mischief. 'I should have brought her something better than a bag of sweets,' she reproached herself. 'She's probably engaged to Malachy Boland by now – something personal like a leather purse or a signet ring.'

A taciturn woman with long hairs growing out of her nose arrived and Miss Higgins banished her sentimental notions to give her the whole of her attention.

'Maybe she's married already. She could be on her honeymoon.' By the third day she was growing weary of the view from her window. She made it a rule never to discuss clients but when a young girl, about the doe's age, came into her room with towels, it seemed a natural thing to mention her favourite.

'What do you know?' the youngster sat down on the bed. 'She's gone into the convent. She's after getting the call. Now who'd have thought such a thing of Maisie Quilligan that was mad as a March hare?'

'What about Malachy Boland?' Miss Higgins looked out at the sea.

'Ah, him! Gone on the boat from Cobh. He was all out for himself – gave Maisie the push. She was gorgeous too, wasn't she? She used to be gorgeous. Did you know her? Only she suddenly developed this crop of bristles all over her face and neck. Like a warty hog.' The girl gave a snort of laughter.

When the chambermaid left her, Miss Higgins ate the Lemons' Pure Sweets one by one, until the boiled confections bit into her tongue and blistered it. The pain would bring tears to your eyes.

'Nice cup of tea,' she told herself kindly. But she stayed where she was, smiling out the window at the prankish waves.

# A Model Daughter

'Think!' said my friend Tilly one day when we were deep into a bottle of lunchtime Meursault; 'if we had had children when we ceased to be impervious virgins they would be seventeen by now. Seventeen or thereabouts. Lovely girls!'

For a moment before her words misted into grapey vapours I could see them sitting opposite us with shiny hair and loose frocks of Laura Ashley prints.

In her early youth Tilly had been very fast and a famous mistress. She was slower now and more faithful and our friendship was occasionally shadowed by a creeping sentimentality that made me fear she would one day rush away from me and into the arms of Jesus.

'Do you regret not having had children?' I said briskly.

'I would like a girl.' She was stubborn: 'Seventeen or so.'

'You could have one. You still could.' She was forty-five but friendship entitled her to lay claim to my age, which was not quite forty.

'Have one what, darling?' Her beautiful blue eyes always had the attractive daze of myopia but after lunch and wine they shimmered under a sea haze.

'A baby!'

'A baby?' She recoiled as if someone had just thrust a seeping member of the species on to her silk knee. 'Don't be revolting!'

'Babies are where children come from,' I pointed out; a little shortly, for I had a worry of my own.

'Not necessarily,' Tilly said. 'It seems to me absurd to go to such lengths. There are young girls everywhere. In primitive countries people drown them at birth. Still they outnumber the men.' She seized the bottle and shook the dregs, very fairly, into either glass. 'If I feel the need of a daughter, I daresay I can get one somewhere.'

'But where?'

Her confidence was shaken but only for a moment. 'A model agency!'

I had a daughter. It was my one secret from Tilly. Her name was Hester and she was seventeen. My daughter was born not of love, not even of sex, but of necessity. I married Victor when I was twenty and we were both pretending to be actors, knowing perfectly well that one day we would have to grow up and get ourselves proper jobs. Six months later, to everyone's surprise, he got a break and was summoned to America. He fell in love, to no one's surprise, with his leading lady. The divorce was quick and uncontested. Shamed by my failure I kept my mouth shut and my head down. I got a small settlement and descended into that curious widowhood of the heart which an early broken marriage brings.

I was too lethargic to work and faced a frugal living on my mean allowance. 'If you had a child,' my mother scolded, 'he would have to pay a proper maintenance.' Even in this I had failed. 'Well I can't just manufacture a child!' I cried. Mother made a face, as if tasting some invisible treat inside her mouth. 'Pity,' she said.

'Dear Vic,' I wrote, alone in my little room by the gas fire. He no longer seemed dear to me. I had grown sullen and immune to attachments. 'I did not want to tell you this earlier as I had no desire to destroy your happiness as you have mine, but I am expecting our child. I am letting you know now only because money is short and it will be so difficult to work.'

Vic was generous. He was a successful actor now and relieved by my faint-heartedness. A card arrived, offering congratulations, and a decent-sized cheque which was to be repeated monthly.

I didn't bother Vic much after that except in due course to announce that Hester had been born and from time to time when I badly needed a bit of extra money (for a furry coat in a really dreadful winter; for a Greek cruise because Tilly was urging me to accompany her) and then I would say that Hester had a little illness or needed her teeth straightened or that she was plaguing me for pony lessons. Once, after his second marriage had broken up, he wrote and asked if he could come and meet Hester. After a momentary panic I answered with a very firm 'no'. I had never asked him to come to her side when she was ill, I pointed out. It would be unfair of him to disturb our peaceful lives.

He accepted this, with a sort of written sigh. 'Just send me a picture of her,' he said. I was shaken, but underneath the dismay there grew a kind of excitement. I said earlier that I had grown immune to attachments. In fact it was merely romantic attachments to which I was resistant, and my friend Tilly consumed enough sexual adventure for both of us. I had a deep secret attachment to my Hester. As soon as Vic asked for her picture I realized that I too had longed to know what she looked like.

I began to carry a camera around. I sought Hester in restaurants, outside schools, in bus queues. One day I was seated in the park in the shade when a child came and looked at me; a solemn dark-eyed girl with a pink dress and a little shoulder bag of white crochet work. I snapped the child and smiled at her. She stood, quite still and graceful, fulfilling her role. I closed the shutter on my camera and closed my eyes too, to carry the moment past its limits so that she came right up to me and called me Mama. When I looked again, the girl was gone.

I wonder how often Victor looked at the picture I sent him, if he kept it in his breast pocket close to his heart; if he placed some of his hopes on that unknown child. I know I did. It helped to pass a decade swiftly and quite sweetly. Soon I was heading up to forty, the extremes of my youth gone (but not regretted) and I found myself thinking idly that Hester would be leaving school by now and we might be planning her college years. I liked this fantasy for the placing of Hester in Oxford or Cambridge would make her actual absence more plausible and allow me to enjoy my dreams with no disturbance from the dull utilities of fact.

'Dear Vic,' I wrote. 'It is some time since I have been in touch but the years have flown and we were so busy, Hester and I, with work and school, that we had no time to consider the world outside our own little one. However, the news now is too big to keep to myself. Our girl has won a First to Oxford. I want you to know that I sustain no bitterness in regard to our marriage for Hester has been a true compensation. I only wish I could indulge her with all the silly clothes students love and a little flat of her own where she could invite her grown-up friends for coffee.'

It would have been a better letter (I would have been a better person) without the embellishment of that final sentence but the truth is I got carried away and there really was a nice little flat which Tilly had been urging me to snap up.

Vic wrote back immediately. 'Wonderful news! Of

course my daughter shall have everything she wants but this time I am determined to deliver it (and my congratulations!) in person.' He announced a date when he would arrive and named the restaurant where we would meet for a celebration dinner.

I suffered several moments of deep shock before my brain broke into demented activity. How should I forestall him? My first thought was a death. Hester dead in a tragic horseback accident! But he would want to see her burial place. Besides, I could not bear that loss myself. I could say she had gone abroad with friends for the summer. Vic was rich. He would insist on following her there.

Nothing I could think of was any use. All my little plans fell apart in the face of Victor's strength of purpose and superior cash flow. Besides, I did not entirely want to put him off for there was the bait of Hester's pocket money. I felt it was a point of honour to collect it safely.

On several occasions I was tempted to confide in Tilly but Tilly is like a viper on the subject of superficial friendships and I knew she would find it impossible to forgive my years of concealment. However, I stuck close to her in those worrying weeks, hoping that I might find the courage to blurt it all out or that she might inadvertently produce an anecdote or experience which would prove the solution to my dilemma. It was exactly four days before Vic's arrival that Tilly, in vino, produced her unlikely veritas of maternal regret and provided me with an answer.

A model agency! I had often glanced through fashion magazines when goaded by Tilly into visiting a hairdresser and I knew those purveyors of fantasy by sight. I was not especially interested in clothes so I gave my attention to the girls who showed them. Unlike Tilly, I did not envy them their taut busts and tiny backsides, their perfect skin and carefully arranged clouds of careless hair. It was their determination that made me wistful.

Their qualification, apart from beauty, which can be used or abused in so many ways, was epitomized by an enduring personality which helped them adhere to a diet regime of meagre, proteinous scraps, to drink prickly Perrier instead of easeful gin, to go to bed at ten o'clock rather than allow themselves to be lured on some exciting, promiscuous prowl. It was more or less how I had pictured Hester.

All I needed was a sweet young girl to help me through a single evening. I know Victor. His passions are burning but brief. Once he had met his daughter, he could peacefully forget all about her.

'I want a girl,' I told the telephone of the Modern Beauties Agency and I gave it the date; 'just for an evening.'

'Daywear, beach or evening?' said a voice.

'Just a simple dinner dress.' I was slightly taken aback.

'Own shoes or shoes supplied?'

'One was rather hoping she might have a pair of her own.'

'Size and colouring?'

I could be confident about this, at least. I described Hester as seventeen or thereabouts, tall but slim, with dark hair and a lily-pale skin.

'It's Carmen Miranda you want,' the telephone decided. 'Will you require a hairdresser and make-up artiste?'

'Carmen Miranda? Now wait a minute!'

'Thirty-five pounds an hour and VAT. To whom shall I make out the invoice?'

'Thirty-five pounds? But . . .! Heavens!' I had anticipated that beauty might be remunerable at about four times the rate of skilled professional housework. I had put aside £50 for the evening. At this price it would cost about £200 – an impossible sum.

'Do you want to confirm that booking or make it provisional. Miss Carmen Miranda is our top professional model. She is very much in demand.'

'No! I mean, yes, I'm sure she is. The thing is, I don't think I have made myself quite clear.' I explained that I did not really require the services of their top professional model. What I wanted – *needed*, was an ingénue, an unspoilt young girl with little or no experience. And cheaper.

'The rate is standard,' said the voice, with a new, steely edge. 'Unless, of course, you want one of our new girls who have not yet completed their training.' She mentioned something that sounded like Poisoned Personality Course and added that these incomplete models could be rented hourly at a reduced rate of twelve pounds, for experience.

'Yes, yes,' I said eagerly. 'That's just right. A young girl, barely out of school. That sounds lovely.'

'All our girls are lovely.'

'I'm sure they are. Thank you so very much. You've got the description?'

'Yes, that's no problem.'

'You've been very kind. Can you tell me who to expect?'

'I'll have to see who's free.'

On the evening of our meeting I felt more excited than on my first date with Victor. Acquiring Hester's childhood photograph had been a rewarding experience. Now I was to meet her in the flesh.

I was looking forward to seeing Victor too. I had often watched him on the television and was intrigued that his face, with its strange orange American tan, had not aged at all while his eyes had, so that he looked like a spaniel with a bulldog's gaze. 'Tricky Vicky', Tilly called my ex-husband but his unreliability did not bother me now; I wanted to hear about his exploits and to be praised for my achievement – Hester – and I was looking forward to getting some of his money. The evening had acquired an additional significance. We would meet as a successful family, untouched by the tension, the sacrifice, the quelling of self that normally accompanies family life. We had got off scot free and yet would not be exposed in loneliness.

I checked with the agency to make sure that my surrogate daughter was still available and they, wearily, assured me that Angela or Hazel or Patricia would meet me in the lounge at the appointed hour. Such nice names! Nothing could go wrong. All my little Angela or Hazel had to remember was to answer to Hester. There were no shared memories to rehearse. Vic had no experience of academic life so she would not be quizzed on that. In any case I had taken the precaution of booking the girl half an hour in advance of Vic's arrival time so that I could give her a little briefing.

It was almost that time when I was startled by the arrival in the lounge of a sort of human sunburst. Women started to wriggle and whisper. 'Good Lord,' I said ungraciously. It was Vic, thirty-five minutes early.

He cast his gaze over the women in the lounge, not really looking for me but allowing each female present to melt and open to his boyish charm. Perhaps he would not recognize me. I could slip out and wait at the exit for Hester to prime her on her role. I rose, face half averted – and drew attention to myself.

'Barbara!' His voice had gained boom and timbre. He put a little kiss on the air and flopped down casually beside me, fastidiously raising the knees of his trousers.

'Hello Vic.'

'Sorry I'm so early. First night nerves,' he said, his nose wincing appealingly under his drooping eyes. He had developed an American accent.

'That's all right. Have a drink.'

'You look good,' he said. 'How's life been treating you? What a time I had, getting here! You would think, since we were shooting in Europe . . .' And he launched, as I had imagined he would, into a story about himself.

When Hester comes, I shall rush to the door to greet her, I thought. I gave Victor my smiling mouth and my nodding head but my attention was elsewhere. I shall see a tall, pale, beautiful girl — probably shy — in the entrance and I shall run to her and put my arms around her and if she doesn't cry out for help I shall just have time to explain before we get back to the table.

Something Victor said brought my mind right back. '. . . Anyway, I'm glad I got here early so we could talk about money before Hester gets here.'

'Money?'

'A sort of financial plan. I thought, twenty thousand dollars now, or five thousand a year until she's twenty-one. If you take the lump sum now you could invest it but there's less risk with an annuity.'

'Twenty thousand dollars?' My head spun as I tried out a string of noughts against the little digit and attempted to perform a dollar conversion.

'Well, I guess that's not a lot these days. What the heck — make it pounds.'

'Oh, Vic. I'm very — she'll be very grateful.'

'Say, what's she like?' Vic leaned forward and touched my knee.

'Quiet. More like me than you, I'm afraid. I hope you won't be disappointed.'

'I've been disappointed since.' The bulldog eyes attempted bashfulness. 'I wasn't disappointed then.'

We were getting along quite nicely when a wretched autograph hunter recognized Vic and hovered at his chair. She just hovered but her presence sapped one.

'Look, dear, if you don't mind . . .!' I said.

The girl glared at me. I flinched in the dull light of those purple-ringed eyes set in a yellowish face and crowned with gluey horns of hair. She wore a cheap Indian cotton anorak and an extraordinary satin dress from which her uncooked-looking breasts popped unpleasantly. Quite suddenly, tears bubbled up in her eyes. 'Aw shit,' she said and she tottered off. She did not leave the room. Her perambulation took her in the opposite direction where she paused, glancing back. Vic and I laughed uneasily and he called a waiter for champagne. He was appraising the label when the girl returned and crouched beside me, breathing wetly and heavily in my ear: 'Look, are you Mrs Marshall?'

'I am.'

'Well I'm Araminta.'

Victor was staring.

'Look here, dear . . .'

'From the agency.'

'What?'

'My real name's Angela. Araminta's my professional name — going to be.'

'No!'

'What's the matter?' Victor said.

'I think she's sick or something,' said Araminta.

'Sick!' I echoed faintly. It was not a lie. I rose and bundled my arms around the repellent Araminta. 'Please excuse us.'

Araminta and I faced each other in the uneasy pinkness of the ladies' washroom. 'You must leave immediately,' I said. 'There has been a dreadful mistake.'

'Who says? Whose mistake?' Her voice was a whine.

'You were brought here tonight to represent my daughter Hester, to celebrate with her famous father — whom she has never met before — her scholarship entrance to Oxford University.'

'That's beautiful. Like an episode from "Dallas".'

'If you think, for one instant, that you are fit to stand in the shoes of my daughter then you are even more deranged than you look. Now go away!'

'Here!' Her wail was like a suffering violin string. 'I want my money.'

'Not a penny!'

Araminta's mouth opened into a grille shape and a loud gurgle of grief issued therefrom. 'It's not my fault. No one told me I was to be your frigging daughter. I borrowed money to have me hair done an' all. What am I going to do?'

I was pondering the same question when the door opened, and Vic came in, looking confused. 'Is everything all right? Who's this?' he said of the screaming, streaming Araminta.

My soothing utterances were lost in the noise that Araminta made, of a train reversing, to sniff back her sobs. Her face was striped with purple but erased of tears. 'Hello Dad,' she said. 'I'm Hester.'

We were all congealed like the victims of Pompeii. After an eternity of seconds Vic showed signs of recovery. 'Hester?' he whispered. 'Barbara . . .?'

I closed my eyes. I could not look at him. 'She is going through . . . a phase.'

I heard a tap running, a tiny strange bark of dismay as, presumably, some woman attempted to enter and found her path blocked by a famous heartthrob. When I could bear to look I saw Hester calmly splashing her face, applying fresh scribbles of purple to her eyes and daubing her lips with mauve gloss that resembled scar tissue. Poor Vic looked badly shaken. On an impulse I seized the girl and ducked her beneath the tap again, washing every trace of colour from her skin. I scrubbed her dry on a roller towel and then patted her complexion with my own powder puff and a smear of my blusher. Her eyes, even without their purple tracing, resembled Mary Pickford's in their worse excesses of unreasoned terror. 'You some kind of frigging maniac?' she hissed. 'Shut up!' I wielded a hairbrush which I used to remove the glue from her head, and some of her hair. When I had finished there stood a tall, pale girl with wild dark hair, a little overweight, quite pretty, although her eyes and her breasts still popped nastily.

Whatever Vic was feeling he used his actor's training to conceal it. 'Come along, girls,' he said. 'It doesn't do for an actor to get himself arrested in the ladies' loo!'

Hester cawed with mirth.

Back in the restaurant there was a period of peace while Hester ate and Victor brooded. The girl appeared to be ravenously hungry. She did not pay any attention to us until a first course and several glasses of wine had scuttled down her throat and her cheeks were nicely padded with roast beef and then, with a coy, sideways look at Vic, she produced a classic line:

'Where have you been all my life?'

Vic eyed her gloomily. 'Hasn't your mother explained?'

'Not bloody much.'

Odd that I had not noticed before that they both had the same pessimistically protruding eye.

'I think your mother has rather a lot of explaining to do,' Vic said.

'Pardon?' I was so startled I could only squeak.

'Barbara, I am disappointed.' He put up a hand to swat a second squeak of protest which was escaping.

'Yes! I have been let down. Over seventeen years I have given unstintingly to the support of my daughter, trusting that you would bring her up as I would wish. You denied me access to her. I did not attempt to use the force of law in my favour. You did not want your lives disturbed, you said. What life? I ask you, what life have you given this girl? It is clear from her speech that she has been allowed to run wild in the streets. She's even hungry. Look how she eats! Have you anything to say?'

Very little, really. It was true the girl was appalling. 'Just be glad you haven't had to put up with her,' I snapped.

'She won't give me my money,' Hester complained. She shoved another roast potato into her mouth and seized Victor's sleeve. 'You'll give me my money, won't you?'

Victor retrieved his garment. 'Young lady, I'll give you something more valuable than money. I will give you advice. Reach for the moon – not its reflection in some puddle in the gutter. Look beyond the superficial values of youth and fashion. Stand up proud – alone if needs be. You'll have self-respect. You'll have *my* respect. What do you say, dear?'

'Vic,' I interjected, lost in our improvised drama; 'it is you who must look beyond the superficial. She has won a First to Oxford.'

'I'm not talking to you, Barbara. I'm speaking to my daughter. You know I don't believe the academic world equips you for real life. Now Hester, what do you say?'

'Why don't you ride off into the sunset on your high horse, you big ballocks?' Hester said, and she importuned a waiter for profiteroles.

Victor looked so stunned, so *dis*armed, I was almost sorry for him. 'She is overwrought,' I said. 'Think what she has achieved! She has been locked up with her books all year and now she is in . . . revolt.'

Underneath I had begun to warm to Hester. Victor was not used to challenge. My once-husband seemed quite broken by her reproach. 'You know I don't expect much,' he sighed. 'It's the simple things I like in women – feminine grace, charm and wit.'

'I'm with you, mate!' Hester spoke up through a mouthful of gunge. 'This university lark was all her idea. Personally I've always thought women would be better off burning their brains than their bras. Could I have a liqueur?'

'You mean you don't want to go to university?' I was quite hurt.

'Too bloody right. I'm really a model, you know,' she confided to Vic. 'Although what I'd like best in all the world . . .' (her eyes glittered greedily) '. . . is to be an actress.'

'You'd like to be an actress?' Vic threw me a tiny look of triumph. His expression began to brighten.

'Dearest Dad . . .!' She leaned across the table so that her breasts rested on her pudding plate like a second, uncoated helping of dessert and it began to dawn on me that she might be a little bit drunk: 'All my life I have worshipped you from afar. My one dream has been to emul . . . follow in your hallowed footsteps.'

Vic smiled. His bulldog's gaze flickered with warmth and interest. Their eyes, inches apart, wobbled glassily. The child's look grew positively rakish and I had to kick her under the table to remind her of her filial role.

'Chip off the old block!' Vic said in admiration and he patted her pudgy hand.

'Thank you, Daddy.' Hester wrinkled her nose in exactly the way he often does.

'Would you really like to go on the stage?' he said.

'More than anything – except of course, the movies.'

'Then the movies it's going to be. I'm bringing you back with me.'

'No!' I moaned.

'You mean it?' Hester said.

'I can get you a small part in the film I'm working on. Just a walk-on but it will be a start. Come back to America with me and we'll get you into stage school. I'll make Hollywood sit up and take notice of my beautiful daughter.'

Hester glowed so that, in the flattering candlelight, she did look rather beautiful. I felt depressed. Vic was taking my daughter away. There would be no more secret dreams for me; and no more money.

'Of course we'll have to tidy you up a bit!' Victor had advanced to practical planning. 'You're going to have to learn to speak properly and I'm afraid, darling, you'll have to lose some of those curves. First thing tomorrow you're going on a diet. I want you skinny as a stalk of celery before we go back.'

At this Hester's face began to alter shape, the jaw extending, the eyes receding into pink slits, the mouth widening and lengthening. We watched in awe until a horrible howl came out. 'I can't!' she wailed. 'I'm pregnant!'

It was some time before I saw my friend Tilly again. There was such a lot to do with the baby coming and poor Vic in such a state. 'I insist that you tell me everything. Everything!' he had said in the restaurant after Hester dropped her bombshell, and of course the wretched girl did.

She has gone now. I think it's for the best. She ate such a lot and would answer only to Araminta. In any case now that the baby is born it would be confusing to have two Hesters in the house.

In the end Araminta did go back to America with Vic. No longer father and daughter, they had found a new role which seemed to suit both of them much better. And Vic left me really a very generous allowance for the child.

I hope I have explained my story clearly to you for I simply cannot seem to make Tilly understand. 'Good God, darling,' she said, peering with fascinated horror into the pram on the day I introduced her to the infant. 'Did I never tell you about the Pill?'

And there was Hester, so sweet and solemn in her frills, her hands waving like pink sugar stars; her life stretched out before us, its mysterious curves and dazzling prospects, its sunlit patches and shadows, like the carriage drive to some enchanting manor.

I tried once more to tell my friend about my daughter's coming, but Tilly, fearing tales of childbed, waved a dainty hand burdened with costly mineral rocks, and said: 'What matter the source of life so long as it is lived happily ever after.'

She is right of course, for which of us anyway ever truly understands where babies come from.

# Concerning Virgins

These things no longer matter because the house is gone and the people are dead but ghosts only settle when they have got over their surprise and history shows that concerns last longer than matter.

An old man, Narcissus Fitzgall, lived with his two daughters in a house called Herons' Peep on the edge of the water in County Wicklow. It had been built on a hill above the river but appeared, from the inside, to be suspended in water. Water dappled its ceilings with luminous shadow and moved in spotted motion behind the curtains. It gushed darkly underneath the bedroom windows and vanished in a silver trail miles away, between lacy wands of ash. Where the river ended the sea began. There was a stretch of marsh fed by seawater and wild birds nested in giant reeds. Beyond this was a little shingle beach on which to stand in the wind and listen to the soft crumple of the waves and a tempting chatter like glass-beaded curtains as the tide dragged its dead water back across the stones.

The house and its steeds and its birds and its reeds seemed made for pleasure but Narcissus Fitzgall was not a happy man. 'I need a wife,' he sighed. 'God grant me a wife. Sweet suffering souls!' – he damaged his gouty foot upon the martyred rump of a favourite hound – 'it ain't as if I want a cook or a beauty – only a wife.'

He did not need a wife to care for him. His two

daughters, Blanche and Grace, served the old man with silent loyalty. They were aged somewhere between thirty and forty and looked as if they had been washed too frequently – and he detested them.

Although he insisted absolutely on purity in women his personal preference was for a woman you could whack on the behind, whose breasts grew lax in their moorings after champagne and claret. As he grew older his days were poisoned by the constant filial presence. They had developed a preserved look as they began to dry out as if they would live, rustling and dispirited, for ever.

He did not need a wife to soothe his passions. Fancy these days was an irksome intruder whose name he sometimes could not remember. When the need arose, a young scullery maid made less of a compliment and could be dismissed if she grew argumentative. He needed a wife to give him a son. Time was running out. His body had grown unreliable. It had lost interest in his will and seemed embarked on an excavation for its own skeleton, neglecting to send blood to his extremities or to digest the fat of game or the esters of old alcohol. Unless he could soon put a squalling heir to the breast of a woman who bore his name, he must go to his grave in the horrible knowledge that Herons' Peep would fall to the busy, timorous fingers of his daughters.

For all its beauty, Herons' Peep was not a feminine estate. It was a man's house. Unlike most Irish houses, which look stern on the outside and graceful within, it showed all its gentleness in its face. Inside it was handsome but harsh. The uncovered floors answered the stamp of boots. Grates were vast marble maws where whole trees were splintered and consumed. The sofas had been built big enough for a horse or a hound to sleep on, and they did if they liked. Plumbing, when it came, was a series of thunderous geysers and gullets that caused many a superstitious maid to leap from her seat, believing she would be sucked down to the very floor of the ocean below. There were no flowers, no little lamps nor Venice glass. Gilt-framed shepherdesses and darling little painted dogs did not sentimentalize the walls. The kitchen was the very pit of hell, enlivened only by a bright patter of gore from the dripping corpses of the day's sporting slaughter. The river alone was allowed to indulge in female whim, making her music softly on the ceilings – a solitary clemency for many a stolen maid.

In the early days visitors were shocked by the severity of the house and put it down to the lack of a woman's touch. The little girls heard the whispers and assumed this responsibility. As soon as they were able, they hoarded lengths of fabric in their room, begged from neighbours or bought in parish sales, and sewed up assortments of curtains.

Their father locked them in the nursery and fed them boiled rabbit for a week. When they were released, thin and faintly green, they had turned an old velvet ballgown into a set of frilly cushions for a sofa. In spite of Fitzgall's fury they persisted for it seemed as vital to them as salvation to leave the mark of their gender. As little girls deafened by paternal wrath they would hide and cry for their mother. Now when he raged at them they lay down on their beds or stole his spirits and returned gaunter and more enduring. Their nervous fingers never ceased in dainty toil. Although the old man used their finest work to blow his nose or rub down his dogs, the house was sinking under a creeping infection of embroidered samplers.

One day when he was seventy-five he decided that since God would not trouble to send him a spouse, he must get one for himself. He had exhausted his store of charm, influence and menace with all the women in the county, so he resorted to a wise old woman who lived in the local village of Rathwillow and who did a bit of hairdressing in her spare time.

'I need a wife,' he told her.

'What sort of a wife?' She studied him most acutely, as if measuring him up for a suit or a coffin.

'A drudge, a bag, a bat, a hag — any wife so long as she has in her the makings of a boy.'

She kept looking at him, making no comment but holding his eye as if awaiting some response from himself. At length she turned away and observed: 'I knew a man wanted a ferret an' he put a notice in a periodical.' For this, he had to give her a guinea.

All the same, he did advertise for a wife, withholding his name and that of his estate, for he was not a popular man — merely describing himself as handsome, unfettered and rich and offering a box number for reply. After that he had only to add his small requirement in the woman who would fulfil him.

He had been married once to a very beautiful girl called Alice Clements. She was demure and pure as a swan. He went to great efforts to lay claim to her, thundering about the countryside on hunters, shooting pheasants and peasants, spending most of his money on Herons' Peep so that his brothers were left with bare tracts of land to build on. He took her to Paris for her honeymoon and gave her all her heart's desire, and she had treated him abominably. She gave birth to two daughters and showed no repentance. When the younger of the girls was only two she jumped into the river, leaving him in his prime with a house of motherless daughters — and no son.

He sought another wife as soon as possible. He had exhausted his store of sentiment on Alice and formulated more economical styles of wooing.

Sometimes he simply canvassed the parents of an intended with his financial statements. Oddly, the response was poor. He lowered his sights to the landless gentry but even their luckless female tribes resisted him. He offered his fortune to poor, pure peasant girls but they fled into convents or painted their faces with the scars of smallpox. He could not understand it. He was a man of substance; handsome – the blood a bit too close to the skin and the brow too beetling, but a good feast for a hungry virgin.

At first he wondered if he had transgressed the narrow boundaries of county form by resuming courtship a month after his bereavement but a crueller truth emerged. His wife's ghost spoke against him. It was said he had driven her to her death. Her pallid spirit came back dripping from the deep and called him callous – he, who had lavished his fortune upon her and expended his best energies in bringing her to bliss.

When he married chaste Alice, he meant her to become his amorous masterwork, his private whore. Naturally she had repulsed the passionate sieges of his courtship. He could not have married her otherwise. He perceived all virtuous wives as irresistible hypocrites who enjoyed the joke of public modesty and twinkled for their husbands like the stars by night. He introduced his bride to his symphony of connubial themes, inspired by the most expensive houses of London and in the arms of plump, intuitive girls of fifteen, and she gazed at the water patterned ceiling. Her lips, obediently fastened to where he directed them, moved ticklishly in prayer.

So deep was Alice's resistance that Narcissus Fitzgall could not resist it. Instead of leaving her alone to be a good wife and mother, he persisted over the years in tormenting her with different systems of arousal.

Rumour has it (but whoever believes such things?) that at length he brought a serving wench to their bed to demonstrate the true nature of female response. Alice lay mute in muslin cap and shift until, at a point where he was unable to give her his attention, she leaped from the sheets with a small mew, went downstairs with her candle and slipped into the river.

A little bitterness is fitting to the victim of a tragedy. 'How do we look, Father?' said his two young daughters twelve years later as they prepared for their first dance in gowns cut down from the remnants of their mother's wardrobe. 'The woods would be very silent if only the nightingale sang,' their papa sadly smiled. All the same they did well at parties – well enough to make him suspect that some young scoundrels had their minds intent on robbing his female property of their only worthwhile asset. He had no interest in his daughters but he had ambitions for them. He wanted them to marry well. There were good estates within riding distance where advantageous connections might be made for the son he would eventually get. The girls looked fair enough. They had no wens or marks and were growing pretty little figures. All he had to do was keep them safe until they were old enough to marry. He forbade them further dances and banned visitors from the house. He locked up his daughters and had men with dogs patrol his grounds. The girls attempted to smuggle out notes and make secret trysts and gnawed noblemen limped about the county to testify to the fact that they had once been attractive, as Narcissus Fitzgall's dogs had once been vicious.

Fitzgall was getting old. He had forgotten that in order for men and women to marry they have first to meet. Memory had flung out the souvenirs of courtship – the teas and dances and rides and picnics, spread over with lace and perfume and roses and manners, laid under with a thunderous compression of lust.

The girls met no one. Lace flew from their nervous fingers and their lips grew pale. They read and walked and stitched and stitched and took little nips of tonic wine. By the time they were deemed of marriageable age, they already had the look of spinsters. Wicked rumour flourished once more, enclosing them like a wall of brambles. Why had the Fitzgall girls been locked up for years and years? It was said they suffered from the phrensy, that their mother had jumped in the river to quench her candle when the moon was full and had left her orphans a legacy of queerness in the head. When Narcissus Fitzgall put them up with a fair dowry there were no bidders. He was enraged and blamed his daughters for plainness, resenting them more with each sparrow's foot that left its tiny print beneath their downcast eyes.

It was indecent that no man had married them, that he should have to bear the brunt of their unflowered withering. One only put up with older women because of the children they had borne, as an example of virtue to those maturing young. It was insupportable that his lovely, adventurer's house might one day fall to his unclaimed daughters.

Now that he had taken measures to prevent this, he might have grown kinder, but as he awaited a response to his advertisement for a wife, the old man became very odd indeed. Sensing an end to his detestable dependence, he grew spiteful and rash.

He filled the sherry bottle, where he knew the girls helped themselves to secret refreshment, with vinegar, and put hare's blood in the port decanter. He employed a poor thing in the village to make up a series of samplers stitched to his direction and disposed them through the house. He found Grace standing rigidly in front of the one that read: 'If hell is a well of whiskey, oh, death where is thy sting?' Blanche was being timidly sick in the bathroom after an appalling sip from the port decanter.

The poor girls knew nothing of his plans and were alarmed to hear him croaking with cruel laughter in the night. 'Tea, Papa?' Bravely they crept up beside his bed.

'Leave the poor teapot in peace!' he roared at them. 'You have a spinster's preoccupation with little pissing spouts.'

When he had frightened them away he returned to his amusement of imagining the procession of applicants for his marital favours – the lonely, the ugly, the fat. He thought he might choose a very fat one. He enjoyed imagining the hulking brute of a son they would make and what sport he would have with his decrepit siblings. His daughters would flee to some chilly wing of the house where he need never look at them but could, when he remembered, dispatch milquetoast or a little thin soup.

Disappointingly, this pleasure was deferred. When he went to collect his post there was nothing but a begging letter from a widow, pleading for a fragment of his fortune in order to feed her children. After three weeks had passed with no single answer, he consulted the wise woman again.

'Did you maybe set your sights too high?' she wondered.

'I asked for nothing,' he protested, 'not looks, not charm, not money! See!' He handed her a copy of his notice and she read it, her gnarled face slowly unravelling to reveal a blackened pit of mirth. 'You wanted jam on your egg and no mistake,' she cackled, and read aloud:

'Handsome, landed gent of considerable means seeks virgin bride of childbearing age.'

'What proposal could be more modest?' he begged.

'God bless you, sir, and saving your presence, you black-hearted oul' blackguard — with curs like yourself around, where do you expect to find a virgin?'

'Silence, hag! I'll have your head,' Narcissus Fitzgall was infuriated by her impudence.

'Why not, so, since you had my maidenhead more than fifty years ago — not that you'll remember — and that of every other poor girl who had neither man nor money to protect her.

'Forget about virgins now, sir. Look out for a nice widow lady who'll give you a son without even troubling you to father it.'

'The mother of my son must be a virgin.' The old man remained stubborn.

'Give me another guinea,' she said.

He put the money in her hand and she transferred it to her corset and slowly began to write. 'Old man, solvent, wishes to make contact with maiden lady in desperate circumstances, view to matrimony and mutual advantage.'

There were desperate women then as there are desperate women now and always will be. When next he went to inspect his mail a couple of letters awaited him. Having passed the previous month in disappointment he felt exhilarated, spoilt for choice. He determined that one of the authors would be his bride no matter how dire her circumstance, how horrible her impediment. Bad breath would not stand in his way, nor apoplexy nor skin blackened by mercury poisoning, he vowed as he tore open his post and scanned the spinsterish script of two virgins who pleaded to become 'Yours truly . . .'

When the girls found him he had begun to go brittle

and the letters were locked into a mortified grasp. They stooped solicitously to their father's corpse. With barely a glance at one another and only the mildest of sighs, they retrieved their very private correspondence.

# FOR THE BEST IN PAPERBACKS, LOOK FOR THE 🐧

In every corner of the world, on every subject under the sun, Penguin represents quality and variety – the very best in publishing today.

For complete information about books available from Penguin – including Puffins, Penguin Classics and Arkana – and how to order them, write to us at the appropriate address below. Please note that for copyright reasons the selection of books varies from country to country.

---

**In the United Kingdom:** Please write to *Dept E.P., Penguin Books Ltd, Harmondsworth, Middlesex, UB7 0DA.*

If you have any difficulty in obtaining a title, please send your order with the correct money, plus ten per cent for postage and packaging, to *PO Box No 11, West Drayton, Middlesex*

**In the United States:** Please write to *Dept BA, Penguin, 299 Murray Hill Parkway, East Rutherford, New Jersey 07073*

**In Canada:** Please write to *Penguin Books Canada Ltd, 2801 John Street, Markham, Ontario L3R 1B4*

**In Australia:** Please write to the *Marketing Department, Penguin Books Australia Ltd, P.O. Box 257, Ringwood, Victoria 3134*

**In New Zealand:** Please write to the *Marketing Department, Penguin Books (NZ) Ltd, Private Bag, Takapuna, Auckland 9*

**In India:** Please write to *Penguin Overseas Ltd, 706 Eros Apartments, 56 Nehru Place, New Delhi, 110019*

**In the Netherlands:** Please write to *Penguin Books Nederland B.V., Postbus 195, NL–1380AD Weesp*

**In West Germany:** Please write to *Penguin Books Ltd, Friedrichstrasse 10–12, D–6000 Frankfurt/Main 1*

**In Spain:** Please write to *Longman Penguin España, Calle San Nicolas 15, E–28013 Madrid*

**In Italy:** Please write to *Penguin Italia s.r.l., Via Como 4, I-20096 Pioltello (Milano)*

**In France:** Please write to *Penguin Books Ltd, 39 Rue de Montmorency, F-75003 Paris*

**In Japan:** Please write to *Longman Penguin Japan Co Ltd, Yamaguchi Building, 2–12–9 Kanda Jimbocho, Chiyoda-Ku, Tokyo 101*

## BY THE SAME AUTHOR

### Holy Pictures

In the Dublin of 1925 the holy scriptures are about to be superseded by moving pictures. To fourteen-year-old Nan the cinema appears as a miraculous rescue from the confines of her Catholic upbringing. But growing up into a world of immoral, unreliable adults is not easy, and the last year of Nan's childhood moves from the burlesque to the tragic . . .

'Sharp as a serpent's tooth . . . it is a very long time since a first novel of such promise, of such fun and wit and style, has come so confidently out of Ireland' – William Trevor

### A Nail on the Head

Fifteen stinging, erotic tales on the sexual tripwire, each tale sketched with humour and biting perception. At once comic and tragic, the men and women in these stories are forced up against the limitations of love and life.

'Short, painful tales of love's humiliations' – *The Times Literary Supplement*

'Drawn with a fiercely imaginative, original and accurate hand' – *New Statesman*

### Last Resorts

Harriet loved Joe Fisher for his ordinariness – his suits and hats, his ordinary money mind – even his wife. She had brought up her three children alone. She had forced herself to take the succession of lovers who had fed her urges and her wavering *amour-propre*. And all the time, she had longed for an ordinary life – a head beside her on the pillow, ring on her finger and punctual meals . . .

Each summer, armed with her easel and her children, she decamps to the Greek island of Keptos. This year, she has lured out Joe – promising herself a sun-drenched, wine-stippled interlude of loving and wooing . . .

'An unmitigated delight. Boylan is a true and vibrantly entertaining writer' – *Time Out*

# BY THE SAME AUTHOR

**Black Baby**

On the day of her First Communion, Alice had paid the nuns half a crown to adopt a black baby from the mission in Africa. Mysteriously, the longed-for baby never arrived . . .

Fifty years on, Dinah turns up on Alice's doorstep. Unnervingly black, bawdy and splendid, her leather skirt curving like an iron cooking pot, her red high heels clicking, Dinah holds Dublin in the palm of her hand. And for Alice – in Clare Boylan's gorgeous and blithely comic novel – she spells the beginning of dreams come almost true.

'Splendidly original and richly comic . . . the writing is a joy' – *Irish Times*

'Humorous and inventive . . . it spills over with affections for strangeness and wayward warmth' – *The Times*

'The book I have read with the greatest pleasure, amusement and deep sympathy' – Molly Keane in the *Sunday Times* Books of the Year.